Adachi and Shimamura

STORY BY **Hitoma Iruma** ART BY **Non**

NOVEL
6

When you need to think for a while, fishing's your best bet, or so I was told. But...did I have anything to think about?

"Hmmm..."

For some reason, Adachi came to mind. Maybe I saw a common thread between her and the dog sleeping wearily beside me. She always looked so defeated whenever things didn't go her way... She was the kind of girl who wore her heart on her sleeve, which I could appreciate. It really helped me understand her.

If I were to sum it up, Adachi just...didn't have much experience dealing with people. But that was exactly what made her so interesting to me. Speaking as someone whose overexposure to social interaction had left me numb to it, she was my polar opposite...and every now and then, I found myself tempted to protect her the way I wished someone would have protected me.

Shimamura

A girl with a bit of a ditzy side. Currently visiting her grandparents for the summer. Has been thinking more about Adachi ever since their fight.

Adachi

She has a slim, stick-figure body type with few curves. Has feelings for Shimamura and can't wait for her to come home.

"Hey, you should send me a picture."

"Wh-what? A picture of what?"

"Your swimsuit!"

"Wh-wh-why, though? What for?"

"I want to see you wearing it, silly."

"Ha ha ha ha! Thanks. Pretty eye-catching, I gotta say. So where do you want to wear your new swimsuit? The beach? The river? The swamp?"

"...The bathhouse."

"Oh... Thanks. You look pretty too!"

"Th-thanks...!"

Table of Contents

Adachi and Shimamura

NOVEL 6

STORY BY
Hitoma Iruma

ILLUSTRATED BY
Non

Airship

Seven Seas Entertainment

ADACHI TO SHIMAMURA VOL. 6

© Hitoma Iruma 2016
Edited by Dengeki Bunko
Illustrations by Non

First published in Japan in 2016 by
KADOKAWA CORPORATION, Tokyo.
English translation rights arranged with
KADOKAWA CORPORATION, Tokyo.

Seven Seas press and purchase enquiries can be sent to
Marketing Manager Lianne Sentar at press@gomanga.com.
Information regarding the distribution and purchase of
digital editions is available from Digital Manager CK Russell
at digital@gomanga.com.

Follow Seven Seas Entertainment online at
sevenseasentertainment.com.

TRANSLATION: Molly Lee
COVER DESIGN: Nicky Lim
LOGO DESIGN: George Panella
INTERIOR LAYOUT & DESIGN: Clay Gardner
COPY EDITOR: Meg van Huygen
PROOFREADER: Stephanie Cohen
LIGHT NOVEL EDITOR: Nibedita Sen
PREPRESS TECHNICIAN: Rhiannon Rasmussen-Silverstein
PRODUCTION MANAGER: Lissa Pattillo
MANAGING EDITOR: Julie Davis
ASSOCIATE PUBLISHER: Adam Arnold
PUBLISHER: Jason DeAngelis

ISBN: 978-1-64827-262-2
Printed in Canada
First Printing: August 2021
10 9 8 7 6 5 4 3 2 1

1. Bittersweet Memories

"WHENEVER YOU CHALLENGE yourself, you must always try your hardest. Otherwise you'll never discover what you're truly capable of."

Wise words from a junior high school teacher whose name I couldn't quite remember. I just wish someone would have told me a little sooner. By junior high, all traces of the old me had vanished. I was a carefully polished stone flowing through the river of time. Put nicely, you could say I was free from all restraint. Alternatively, from a less-than-generous perspective, there was nothing keeping me grounded.

That was the kind of girl I had become.

There wasn't any sort of major event that caused it either. After I transitioned from elementary school to junior high, a lot of the people around me simply started being very *specific* about the way they treated others. If you ask me, I merely adapted to that change.

Kindness approached the heart by knocking on the front door, whereas malice crept in through the windows. And when you were innocent and trusting, you generally left your windows wide open. But when it was your own naivete that made everything worse, no one felt sorry for you and no one came to your rescue.

Thankfully, I managed to realize these things before anyone ever hurt me. So I got out my hammer and nails and boarded up every last one of those openings. That way no malice could ever get in...and I could never get out.

Admittedly, when I closed off the door, I seemed to lose my ability to express interest in anything, but at the same time, I never had to expend any energy caring about anything either. It was easier to simply exist in the background. I didn't think of it as good or bad—it was just the way of the world, like the warmth of summer and the chill of winter.

In that sense, I was still the same naive little girl who took everything at face value. Hence I never questioned myself. Instead, I believed that this was how I would always be...and so far, I was still waiting to be proven wrong.

I was complacent. No matter who I met, or how badly I screwed up, or how far my dreams seemed to slip away from me, it didn't feel right to get all clingy about it. As long as I kept my eyes averted, the pain and regret would fade away eventually, and I could go back to my regular self. That was what always worked for me in the past.

But after I met Shimamura, I could no longer avert my eyes. I could no longer afford to be complacent. There was no safe refuge where I could stop and set up camp, so instead, I had to stay on my toes at all times. It felt like I was swimming upstream with the whole current against me...but I could see something beautiful just up ahead.

So in the spirit of pure spontaneity, I invited her to hang out.

"Hang out? Nope, not happening!" Shimamura waved a dismissive hand, yanking the rug out from under me. Then, as I struggled to recover, she explained: "See, my family always spends the Bon Festival at my grandparents' house."

This was a perfectly sensible explanation, and I was faintly relieved to learn she wasn't rejecting me specifically. As someone with minimal family connections, I'd forgotten that most people generally spent this time of year with their relatives.

"Oh."

I should have called ahead of time, but...after that fight we had a while ago, phone calls were kind of scary for me now. Plus, part of me was satisfied just getting to see her face in person. *Ugh, I'm so easily placated.*

"And as it happens, today's the day we leave."

"Right, yeah. I mean, it's the Bon Festival and all."

This was the best response I could think of, and it still came out pointless and vapid. Entirely unrelated, Shimamura was wearing a shirt covered with cartoon eggs, or rather, bizarre creatures hatching out of cracked chicken eggs. Where would she even get a shirt like that? Because I was pretty sure they didn't sell it at the Shimamura Company.

"How long are you staying?" I asked, wiping my sweaty palms.

"Four days and three nights, my lady," she answered, gesturing with her palm up, almost like she was a butler.

"Th-then...could I come back four days from now?" I mumbled shyly, sneaking a peek at her expression.

"Sure, that works," she nodded. As she spoke, she gazed at my face. Then she seemed to sense something and added: "Umm...I'll call you when I get home?"

"I'll be waiting."

Truth be told, I would have given anything to spend those four days camping out in her room.

Just then, I noticed her scrutinizing my neck and forehead. I froze and looked back at her in confusion. Then she walked off down the hallway. Baffled, I waited anxiously until she returned a few seconds later with a bottle of mineral water and an ice cream bar.

"Since you already came all this way, consider this your...hmm... Would it be rude to call it a consolation prize?" She tilted her head. "Your 'come back later' prize? Doesn't have a great ring to it... Your 'pr-ize cream'? Ugh, now it doesn't make any sense..."

Just like that, she was suddenly overanalyzing it. Normally, she never cared about anything, so it was really weird to encounter something she actually dug her heels in about. But to an extent, it was that enigmatic side of her that drew me in.

"Eh, I guess it doesn't matter. Here you go."

With a smile, she tossed her entire train of thought into the trash and handed me my, uh, *prizes*. Instantly, my eyes burned hot. I always reacted dramatically to the smallest things, enigmatic or not... To put it bluntly, I was drawn to *everything* about Shimamura.

Before she could question why I was so enraptured, I quickly ran a hand over my face to compose myself, then took the water and the ice cream bar. Both were cold to the touch, soothing my sweaty palms.

"Don't grip it too tightly or it'll melt," she chided me, and I got so flustered, I nearly dropped the ice cream. Fortunately, I managed to hold onto it—firmly but not tightly. I raised it and the water bottle to eye level.

"Thanks."

"Oh, no worries!" Another dismissive wave.

Then her parents showed up, so I bowed politely, then hurried out of their house. The second I stepped outside, however, reality came crashing down on me, and the warmth I felt from Shimamura's presence was replaced by the intense heat of the sun. But her kind gesture remained securely in hand, nice and cold.

I raised the bottle and gazed at the sky through the lens of the mineral water. Then I thought back to the gym loft. That was where it all began—where this brand-new me was born. Not that I was particularly attached to the old me; for that matter, I couldn't even remember what I was like yesterday. All that mattered was that today's version of me—and tomorrow's, and the next day's—yearned for Shimamura.

So I twisted off the cap and began to drink—not to wash away the old memories, but to water this small sapling.

Gulp by gulp, I chugged down the waterfall.

As I watched her go, it occurred to me that Adachi probably didn't have any family traditions regarding the Bon Festival. If I had to choose, I'd say she was more of a city girl, surrounded on all sides by hard steel. Clean and cold, like she'd never touched dirt in all her life. That was the kind of vibe I got.

And the steel thing explains why she gets overheated so easily, I nodded to myself, even though it didn't entirely make sense.

"We're about to head out, so go get ready," my mother told me.

"Okaaaay..."

When I returned to my room, I found Yashiro lying on my blanket, slowly savoring an ice cream bar. Whether she got it from our freezer or brought it in from somewhere, I couldn't tell. For a moment, I mused to myself idly that her hair looked even more refreshing than the ice cream... Then I belatedly realized she was going to drip it all over my dang blanket.

I reached out and grabbed her by the neck. Despite being a total weakling, I managed to lift her whole body with one arm. She looked back at me, flailing her limbs in mid-air. "What is the meaning of this, Shimamura-san?"

"You promised me you wouldn't eat food on my blanket! Remember?"

"No, I don't."

"Oh, was that my sister…? Whatever. From now on, it applies to you too!"

I carried her safely away from my blanket, then set her down. She walked up to me and leaned her weight against my legs; I knelt down into a sitting position, and she plopped onto my lap. She liked to do this all the time, but oddly enough, she never made me feel overheated. With her color scheme, she looked like a cool breeze.

Grinning, she offered me her half-eaten ice cream. "Would you like a bite?"

"Nom." *Yes, I would.* Sure enough, as I expected from the color, it was strawberry flavor. "Mmm, that's good."

"I know, right?" she replied smugly, as if she'd made it herself.

Come to think of it, the one I gave Adachi was strawberry too. Adachi and Shimamura: Strawberry Flavor… Eh, I guess it wouldn't be noticeably different. All that aside, I started pinching Yashiro's cheeks.

"Hmmm…"

As I kneaded and stretched her soft, flabby skin, I gazed down at her. She was quite possibly the least complicated person in my life. I didn't feel like I had to manage our relationship; even if I messed up, I wasn't worried about doing any real damage. For better or for worse, she didn't take things too seriously. That was probably why people thought she and I were alike: she was always friendly and happy-go-lucky, but there was no real depth to it, like she was just trying it out to see what would happen.

That being said, this laid-back attitude most likely wasn't part of the act.

"Aihheeb!"

She was trying to say something, though I couldn't tell what. *Man, she's so stretchy. Does she even have any bones in here?* I could practically feel the chill of the ice cream through her skin.

"Wha?! Yachi, when'd you get here?!"

"Hello there, Little."

My little sister walked in, and I could see she was sweating, which didn't surprise me since she just went to take her fish tank over to the house next door. My sister was a big-time animal lover, and whenever we went on long trips, she always asked the neighbor lady to feed her fish. *Plus, now she has this new pet to take care of,* I thought to myself as I pinched a strand of Yashiro's hair. It was so sparkly and soft, you could probably make ribbons out of it.

"Would you like some?" Yashiro asked, offering the ice cream to my sister next. She took a small bite from the edge, then looked at me.

"Oh, yeah, Dad said we're gonna leave soon."

"Ah, okay. Be right there."

I rolled Yashiro away—"Oh noooo!"—and grabbed the suitcase I'd packed in advance. If we were going abroad for this vacation, like Hino, then this thing would probably be stuffed to bursting. But we were just going to Grandma and Grandpa's house, so I didn't need that much.

Once we made sure we had everything, my sister and I headed for the front door. Our parents were already outside waiting for us.

"Hurry the hell up, you punks!" my mother snapped, like a small-time thug. But this was nothing out of the ordinary, so I ignored her and put my shoes on.

Now then... "Time for all of us to head out. Hint, hint."

We turned and looked at Yashiro, innocently licking her ice cream. She ignored us and kept on licking.

"Uh, hello?" I demanded. She toddled over at a leisurely pace.

"Yes? How can I help you?"

"Don't play dumb, missy!"

Only then did she recognize the entire Shimamura family's imminent departure. When her bright blue eyes widened, they looked like a pair of miniature globes. "Are you all going on an outing together?"

"I'm *afraid* so," my sister replied, mocking Yashiro's usual tone. I nodded in agreement. *Run along, child.*

"Oh, I see."

Apparently, she sincerely hadn't realized until now. You'd think she would have noticed our entire family scrambling around the house, but I guess not.

"Not to worry. I shall protect your humble abode in your absence," she declared, her chest thrust out, her nose raised high in the air.

Evidently, she had arrived at the complete opposite conclusion. *Not happening, kiddo.* With no other choice, I escorted her bodily from the building.

"Why not?!"

"I know it's easy to forget, but you don't actually live here!"

To us, Yashiro was a pet at most. Not that I expected her to do anything more than lay around and sleep, but even then, no sane person would let this child have the run of the house while we were gone. She was lucky we didn't dump her at the neighbor's place with the fish.

"Be a good girl and I'll bring you a souvenir," my sister chided, like a little mom.

"I am always a good girl, for the record!" Yashiro scoffed, oddly offended.

You sure you wanna make that promise? You know they

don't even have corner stores out there, right? They don't even have stoplights. Or cars. Or people... God, what do *they have?*

"......"

The answer: an old friend I had known for ten years now. When was the last time my heart filled with pure, unadulterated joy when I saw him? These days, that joy was mitigated with sadness in equal measure, blanketing my heart in small, hard cobblestones.

"I shall await my souvenir!"

"Be back soon!"

As Yashiro waved us off, we piled into the car. Frankly, it was kind of surreal. As soon as I buckled my seatbelt, however, I felt my phone buzz. It was an email from Adachi. Curious, I opened it.

"What the...?"

The body of the message was a single heart emoji. Did she send it by mistake? No, that couldn't be it. The heart was bright red, like a strawberry... Whatever it signified, it probably meant more than a simple *bon voyage*.

"Welllll..."

Couldn't hurt to accept it, I figured. So I sent a heart back. Then I leaned against the backseat and settled in to enjoy the long car ride.

Like a giant eyelid, the summer sun left me blinded.

I debated whether to add a heart emoji at the end of my message. I put one just to see what it looked like—*Ugh, it's so obvious! She'll totally notice!*

But when I tried to delete it, I accidentally deleted my message instead...and sent her just the heart by itself!

2. The Other End of the Calendar

TO REACH MY maternal grandparents' house, we traveled along the river, heading upstream. You could see it from every road we drove down. And because we always came to visit in the summer, the sunlight would always glint off the water's surface directly into my eyes. Somehow I forgot about it every year.

It was the same old river, but the water was perpetually changing, like the flow of time itself. *Maybe I've gotten a little taller,* I mused to myself, chin in hand.

We traveled from the dry countryside *waaay* out to the boonies, where everything smelled fresh and earthy. This was still the same prefecture, and yet it already looked nothing like home. We passed over a big, spiraling bridge, then headed along the river once more. Then, around the time the buildings started looking their age and dull mountain colors took over a majority of the scenery, we drove over one more tiny bridge and arrived at Grandma and Grandpa's house.

Their driveway was disproportionately huge—bigger than their whole house, maybe. Atop the poorly drained soil, I could see a depression in the center with a murky puddle of what I assumed was probably rainwater. There were no trees in sight, and yet as we got out of the car, I could hear cicadas wailing at me from every direction. *Talk about surround sound.*

Between the driveway and the house was a thin layer of overgrown vegetation that served as an outside barrier. This was actually the back of the house. It was a lot of hassle to have to walk all the way around to the front door, so for the most part, any relatives that visited would use the back door. At the midpoint, a doghouse with a dingy roof sat empty, no longer in use. I peeked inside just to check, but all that remained of its occupant was a single folded blanket, so I promptly walked away.

As I walked across the bare earth, the heat and scent wafted up from underfoot. This burnt smell always made me feel like I was home again. My vision began to blur like I was underwater...or maybe it was just the summer heat getting to me.

If he died, I would have heard about it by now, so he's still alive, right? Thinking back to how old and weak he looked last year, I followed my parents in through the back door. As we crossed over the threshold, we were met with a gust of cool air.

"I'm hoooome!" my mother called cheerfully.

"Come on in," came the prompt response. "Grandpa's over at the neighbor's house, but he'll be back soon."

There, we were greeted by my grandmother, plus the four-legged resident of the house, lying on the floor. But the second we spotted each other, we both looked up.

"Gon!"

I shot past my mother, calling his name. He was an old dog with missing teeth, poor hearing, and cataracts in his left eye, but he was wagging his tail like he was in good spirits. When I crouched down, he hopped up and hugged me with his full weight, resting his head on my shoulder. I ran a hand along his bony spine in greeting. I only got to see him during the Bon Festival, so this was our yearly reunion. I nuzzled my face against his rough, bristly fur.

"Grrrr. Why does he like you more than me?" my little sister pouted. Since she was the designated animal lover of the family, it was probably a blow to her pride.

"Well, he's known me longer, that's all."

We had first met when we were both little, back when he was first adopted as a puppy, and now he was an old grandpa. Our friendship had spanned a good ten years now.

"He woke up as soon as Hougetsu walked in the door! Must've smelled her," Grandma laughed. She hadn't changed a bit since I was a kid, which was honestly impressive.

Unfortunately, the same didn't apply to Gon. Over the years, he grew bigger and bigger, and then...he grew old. When we were little, he would always jump up to greet me when I arrived; sometimes he'd even pee a little in his excitement. These days, he was much calmer, of course, but I wanted to believe that in his heart, he was still just as thrilled as I was.

My grandparents used to have another dog too, but that one passed away two years ago. Later, I planned to go out and visit his resting place...but once I got there, I could already tell I'd probably start questioning myself again. There was one thing I just couldn't remember for the life of me.

"Oh, Hougetsu, you dyed your hair back!"

"Ow!"

Grandma tugged on a strand of my hair—a small strand, sure, but it still hurt.

"*Nee-chan* finally gave up being a bad kid," my sister announced. Apparently, the mere act of dyeing my hair was enough to label me a delinquent. *Kids these days.*

"Well, that's a shame! You looked better with the lighter hair."

"What, really?" No one had ever complimented my bleach job, other than the hairstylist herself, which...well, of course she would.

"Darn tootin'," she assured me with a grin. *She's totally lying.*

"Oh, they're all here! Sorry, folks. Got caught up in conversation," my grandfather called as he walked in through the front door.

Then another old guy came in after him. This man reeked of dirt so intensely, being in his orbit made me gag. By birth or by sun exposure, his skin was a deep tan color, which contrasted sharply with his bright white beard. He was wearing a blue turban and clothes so baggy, he looked like a desert-dweller. Frankly, I was amazed he could tolerate the heat in all those layers.

Meanwhile, my sister discreetly positioned herself behind me. This man was no stranger to us, but maybe she didn't remember him.

"Well, if it isn't Mr. Iwaya!" my mother exclaimed like a child.

The man smiled at her, eyes crinkling. "Hello there, Yoshika-chan."

"Yoshika-chan"? Never in my life had I heard anyone address my mother like she was five.

"What's that look for?" my mother snapped, quickly detecting my reaction.

"I mean, it's just weird. Aren't you a little old for that?"

"Rude! Hougetsu, you little brat!"

She tugged on my ear from behind; Gon looked at her and barked angrily, which was a real blow to my eardrums, since his mouth was inches from my face. Then it hit me.

"Hee hee hee!"

When I realized Gon had stood up for me, I was so tickled, I started to giggle.

"Hmmm..." My mother pulled her hand away and pressed it to her chin. When I didn't take the bait, she continued of her own accord. "I've got an idea."

"What's that?"

"Wouldn't it be cute to call you 'Houge-choo'?"

Where on earth did that come from?

"Houge...choooo!"

"Ugh! Stop!" Sometimes I really couldn't understand her.

But by the time I looked up again, the two old fogeys had disappeared. "They left to go play mah-jongg,"

Grandma sighed when she noticed me looking around. Evidently, Grandpa was still as free-spirited as ever. Not even a family visit could keep him cooped up at home.

As I smiled, I caught sight of Gon's wagging tail. His fur had seen better days, and energy-wise, he was barely a shadow of his old self.

"Gon..."

Again, I called his name and stroked his back. My chest felt humid on the inside, like my heart was sweating.

Next, we all split up to drop off our luggage. Leaving Gon behind, my sister and I headed to the room allotted to us, which was located on the second floor. It was the first door right next to the narrow staircase; supposedly, it was our mom's old room. It was barely wide enough to fit the bed, which already wasn't that big to begin with, and it was a total pigsty. No one had ever bothered to tidy it up after Mom moved out, I guess.

Directly at the foot of the bed was a closet full of old *Shonen Jump* manga magazines. The closet doors depicted a distant city skyline; at night, when we turned the lights off, I would always stare at it from under the covers and feel at peace. Judging from the beach and the palm trees, maybe it was meant to be a foreign country. Either way, my ordinary life was pretty far removed from either of those things.

"Ugh, I hate this tiny bed."

I always had to share it with my sister, so perhaps it was no surprise that it seemed to shrink and shrink with each passing year. At this point, my sister was probably growing more than I was. *Or am I just getting fat?* I pinched my stomach through my clothes.

"It'd be bigger if you lost weight," my sister remarked boldly.

"Wa ha ha!" Naturally, she received her just deserts for that smart-ass comment.

"Bleeegh..."

Afterward, I left her rolling around on the floor and headed downstairs. When I looked around for Gon, I quickly found him in a dark corner of the airy living room, lying on the floor as if in defeat. His eyes were closed, but when I approached, he slowly looked up at me. I waved to let him know I was just saying hi. He seemed to understand, because he closed his eyes again—peacefully, like the wail of the cicadas didn't even bother him.

It felt like everything in Gon's periphery had lost all color...as if he'd expended all of his energy just celebrating our reunion. *Wow, you must have been really happy to see me, huh? Me too, buddy. At least, I think so.*

I sat cross-legged right next to him, mouth closed, holding my breath, just...sharing my air with him. In the past, there were two dogs around, but now with Gon asleep, there was no one left to fill the house with the sound of barking. The one that passed away was adopted before Gon arrived, so he was even older. But because I first met him when he was a big dog, he didn't take to me quite as much as Gon did.

When I found out that he died, did I cry? This was the one thing that, try as I might, I couldn't quite remember. You'd think there'd be a telltale warmth in my eyes or an ache in my chest, but it just...didn't click. Given this heat, maybe I just couldn't tell the difference between sweat and tears.

"......"

Gon was growing weaker with each passing day. When I first laid eyes on him last year, I started to worry that he might not make it to this year. And now here I was, wondering if he would make it to *next* year.

When Gon dies, will I cry?

Whenever I asked myself this question, something dark and murky clogged my chest, suffocating me.

It felt like I had drawn a raffle ticket that didn't win anything. For the next three days, I would have a zero percent chance of encountering Shimamura on the street. Without that possibility, my life was so *bland*. The whole town was colorless and dead. I didn't even feel like leaving my house.

So instead I sat in my air-conditioned room and agonized over the slowly ticking clock. I would slump forward over the table, then occasionally straighten up again to stave off the restlessness. Three days was an *eternity*...or, more accurately, three days *without Shimamura* was an eternity. Three days *with* her was hardly longer than a blink.

As the boredom and frustration gnawed at me, it became all too apparent that my entire life was centered on Shimamura. That fact in and of itself was fine, but... without her around, I was miserable. My hands fidgeted as I contemplated calling or emailing. But I didn't want to bother her, and besides, I didn't have much to say.

My days off were always exceedingly dull, with nothing worth talking about. Hanging out with Shimamura was easily the highlight of my life...even if it *did* result in me acting like a weirdo half the time. Hard to say if I was making any real progress.

I straightened up and looked at the calendar hanging on the wall. It was completely blank, save for the mark I put on the day of Shimamura's return. Not sure why I bothered putting one at all, frankly, since I wasn't likely to forget, and the sight of it made my chest ache like someone was yanking on my heartstrings.

Next, I paced around and around the room. I was so antsy, I couldn't sit still. It hadn't even been a full day, and already I was desperate to be with Shimamura again.

After a while, I jumped onto my bed and sat cross-legged. Then I fell forward and buried my face in my blanket, turning my vision pitch-black. If only I could spend all three days in this perfect void... I closed my eyes to endure it. But I no longer liked the color black, because now I had learned that something beautiful was waiting for me on the other side of my eyelids.

What colors did Shimamura like? Come to think of it, I still didn't know the answer to what was inarguably one of the most basic questions. My understanding of Shimamura was still riddled with holes. But thankfully, I had the ambition to fill those holes one by one. If I didn't know something, then all I had to do was ask.

Having thought of a topic worthy of discussion, I grabbed my phone and typed out an email that read:

"May I ask what your favorite color is?"

Belatedly, I tilted my head in confusion. *Wait, why did I make it sound so formal?* While I waited for her response, I put my hands in the gap between my crossed legs and swayed from side to side. A short while later, I got an email back that read:

"I like blue and white, I guess?"

"Oh, wow," I murmured aloud. I was expecting her to say she didn't *have* a favorite color, so this came as a bit of a surprise.

Then I thought back to her bleached hair. She really rocked that look... I cursed myself for not taking more pictures of her while I had the chance. But of course, she still looked great with her natural hair, so I decided I would get a selfie with her as soon as she came home.

Ahem. Anyway, blue and white, huh?

I opened my closet to look at my clothes, but I didn't have much in the way of blue, and hardly any white either. Clearly, I would need to go shopping. But if I bought clothes in Shimamura's favorite colors, then maybe we'd end up accidentally matching... Would she remember that I asked and realize I was doing it on purpose? Would it creep her out?

Maybe I could tell her those are my favorite colors too. I hadn't even bought the clothes yet and already I was getting nervous. *God, I'm such a terminal case.*

As far as underwear was concerned, I probably didn't need to worry about the colors. Not like she'd ever have the opportunity to see them...right...? The thought made my brain go all hazy, and I felt the sudden urge to slam my face into the closet door. Instead, I pressed my forehead against it and nuzzled until my skin hurt.

Once I was calm again, I pulled out the swimsuit sitting folded on the edge of the shelf. Thus far, I had only worn it once, but... *Maybe I should go buy another...?* Something told me I wouldn't get another opportunity to go swimming with Shimamura this summer, but...still...

I looked up at the bottom half of the calendar. Summer vacation was only half over, and summer was called "swimsuit season" for a reason. There was no telling where things might lead. Hence, I started thinking maybe it couldn't hurt to be prepared.

Fortunately for me, I had plenty of money to spare, thanks to my part-time job. I had only started working there as a way of killing time, and by this point, I had saved up a decent little nest egg, but I still had no outlet for it. I had no hobbies and nothing I really wanted to save up for. But lately, I had come to understand that this was *precisely* the kind of situation in which that money came in handy. It really felt like I was spending wisely, you know? Yes, this was a very educational experience. Probably.

As it happened, I was scheduled to work today. When the time came, I left the house in the clothes I was already wearing. The instant I walked outside, I was greeted by the drone of the cicadas, though it felt a bit softer today. Summer was already past its peak.

The first half overwhelmed me with its heat, both physically and emotionally...so what was waiting for me in the second half?

I pedaled my bike, miserably sweating up a storm, until at last I arrived at the Chinese restaurant. But when I got there, I found the name of the place had changed. Now there was a *different* dilapidated sign hanging over the entrance. That said, nothing about the interior or the food or the staff had changed whatsoever, so I couldn't really see the point of it. Maybe there was some *feng shui* aspect I was missing. Either way, it gave me bad vibes. Businesses that had to resort to cheap tricks were destined to go bankrupt.

I walked in through the side entrance, then stepped into the office-turned-changing room to get dressed. Only then did I realize: my *cheongsam* was blue. Maybe that was why Shimamura seemed to like it.

Tugging the hem, I walked out to the dining room, and my manager promptly waddled over, followed by a girl I didn't recognize.

"New hire, summer break only. You teach her, okay?"

As the manager spoke, the new girl stepped forward.

Since she was young, naturally, they had put her in a *cheongsam* just like me, except hers was red and embroidered with plum blossoms. And unlike me, she didn't seem embarrassed to wear it—maybe she had embraced the rare opportunity to wear this kind of dress. Oh, and her legs were *ridiculously* long.

"Nice to meet you, Senpai."

"Uhhh…sure."

Before now, all my coworkers were older than me. But then at some point, they all quit, or…got reassigned to some other restaurant, I guess. These Taiwanese-managed restaurants were all buddy-buddy with each other, so it happened all the time, and we lowly employees never got much of a say in the matter. *Wait, but why would they hire a new person when we're hardly ever busy as it is? Or am I just paranoid because of the name change?*

Not like I even really needed this job. I'd already saved up enough "Shimamura money" to tide me over for a while.

"Hey, hey."

My new not-quite-disciple called out to me, so I shot her a questioning look, and she smiled. Now that someone else was wearing a *cheongsam* along with me, I realized just how eye-catching the glossy fabric actually was.

"You don't really seem like you're in charge. Are you younger than me?"

Apparently, she assumed the answer was yes, because she had already dropped all pretense of formality. So I didn't answer...and yet she refused to leave my side.

"Hmmm..." The new "junior" employee put a hand to her chin and tilted her head pensively, and I could feel my hackles rising. "Y'know, kid, I think I might know you from somewhere."

If I had chosen to have this conversation, maybe it would have led to a different story altogether. If I had paid attention to the person in front of me, maybe something would have taken root. But I didn't need any of that.

"Yeah, well, I don't know you."

I shot her down and walked off. Maybe she was just trying to be friendly, but to me, it felt *pushy*—the polar opposite of the comfortable silence I often found with Shimamura. But Shimamura was generally pretty friendly with me too, so what was different? I ruminated on it between customers.

Naturally, the more I thought about Shimamura, the more distracted I became. My imagination spiraled out of control, and try as I might to convince myself I shouldn't walk around smiling like an idiot, it only made me think about her more. It was a vicious circle, as they say. But hey, at least I felt great.

There was a fire inside me that burned hotter than any air conditioning could cool. It was hard to pinpoint exactly what the root cause was—in fact, if I did, it might ruin the whole thing. But somehow I could feel it in my core: Shimamura was the only one for me.

Whenever we went to Grandma and Grandpa's house, we always had the same thing for dinner: pork and chicken cutlets, beloved by Japanese kids everywhere. A giant mountain of them, in fact—and don't forget the miso sauce on top, our local tradition. The mere sight was enough to transport me straight back to childhood. But here in reality, I was already taller than Grandma sitting across from me.

My sister and I pressed our hands together to say grace, and by the time we lowered them, my mother had already started eating. She poured on a ton of miso and stuffed her face like a little kid. But when she grinned at Grandma, I remembered: she *was* their kid. She had spent her whole childhood right here in this house.

"Ahh, I love coming home. This way I don't have to cook," my mother gloated.

"Hey!" Grandma snapped. "Save some for the kids!"

"It's fine, Grandma." Honestly, there was so much on the table, I could already tell we'd be having leftovers for lunch tomorrow.

"We can always make more," Grandpa nodded. At this, we all shook our heads, including my father, who hardly ate much as it was.

If Yashiro were here, she could probably vacuum up an inhuman amount of this food... Was she surviving on her own without us? She didn't break into our house after we left, did she? I felt compelled to keep an eye on her...for multiple reasons. Maybe she was already the Shimamura family pet in my mind.

As I poured the miso sauce over my cutlets, my eyes wandered to Gon lying in the corner of the kitchen, nibbling at some bread that Grandma had crumbled up for him. The amount was so slight, you could mistake it for birdseed, and he was eating it reluctantly, like he was too tired to even chew. In the past, he used to devour anything you gave him and beg for more... Come to think of it, he kinda reminded me of Adachi.

Not that Adachi was quite that annoying, of course. Well, except for when she freaked out at me the other day. She kept babbling on and on, and I couldn't remotely tell what she was trying to express—and she was so emotional,

I didn't dare ask her to repeat herself all over again—so I just kind of...hung up on her. She was sobbing so hard, all her words slurred together, and I could barely parse any of it.

I mean, from *my* perspective, it sounded like:

"I dowa you hag fun thout me! Or holg hansh summer girl—just me! I wayou bewit me! I wand take yufesval myself! I wanbe der why your smiligand have fund! Thasat I wanded! Myad urso much cuz I'bn thinkaba you nostob in loosig my minin...I's wading fyout call! Whydn yever call meer starda cobnsation? Whysit always avabe me? Don you...donya careboume eva liddel? Nothig? Noddeven a bid? Just freds? Jusregur freds? I dowannbe regurfreb—jus wassteb bovat! Thassall I wan... Shibamura, whaddyou wamme do? Well? Shimabura, ayu liddenig? Reay listed. How you feewhen you hemy voidce? Dyou feessomthin? I wand youf feessomthind, anythid, evajus cofford. Thassat I wand. Issat sorong, Shibabura?! Cuz is you! You're the wannawan! I donwan ennyn eld oneed ennyn eld—I onneed you. Is irely so seffisa wan won me's lesteb? Just one! I donc arebout ennyn eld—I don wannem arou—so I'd you? Jusgom fide me adbe wisme ansday wisme andon lead! I donwan ennyn bean wishoe sep me. I wanbe therith you, so jusled me! Hooebe is she? I donnoer. I dowan you turnind some in I donno! I wanno ebthin bout you;

I donwan yookeeb anthin frobme. I haynot noig cuz it heard! It heard so much, Shiamura... I'das you hang out, budeye wannid taykoo fesval. I wandgo wissue, bud yuwenwid her! Ayou hagout wifer? Wherer you rinnow? Ayou wiher, Shigamura? Shiadura, ayou liddenig? Issike I'bin talgindo abbrig wall is hole tibe. Norblyou talga lot more. Why? Whas diberend? Abeye diberend? Yeah, I musbe. Igandell. But I wanno...I wanno bouyou so badiss messinme up. I donwanbe part frob you... I wanbe wisyou ald tibe... I dond gare wheriare long is we're todeth... But I'ven seeyou anni miss you budifee medup ride now I thinguy cry... I ball red grying... I geep wobring hooshies in whashie is do you... Ayou stilidning? Woyou radderbe is her in wime? Abbi nogood enoud? Whappar me is in good enoud? I worgon it, sojusdell me... Iffixit, I swear, so pleajusdell me... I wanno... You're reay spesal me, yunno it? Evif sudwon elsis zakly like youn every way—budere not, soat dozen matter! Jus forgedall that! It hasbe you! I wanus gedalog, but isjus... I wand talk bout moren jus-tice, bud canstob thinkibout it... I me you were smiling! I donwan you smilig enywonnoo isnme! Issucks, yuno? Donyou evefeelike that? Hayou evehadda grush? Dyou haffeeligs someone? Or enywon adall? Dyou knowat lubbis? Somtibe I gescare, wodderig why youste wimme. I mewe freds, anwe? I thig were aleas freds. Dyou thig we freds? Duzit... Hhhnn... Shiabura, say sothig. Lemme heyour voidce. Talk bout me... I wanyou unstan me beddern...beddern enyon. I wanno you, an wanyou know me. I wanyou be my nubber one, ani wanbe yours..."

Needless to say, it felt like someone was pouring overcooked porridge directly into my ear. Still, in hindsight, I could have been a bit nicer about it... Maybe I should have worked up the courage and asked her to repeat it after all.

"Hmmm..."

I mulled it over as I chewed a bite of chicken. It'd be awkward to bring it up again, so the safest option was probably to just forget it ever happened. But something told me that if I procrastinated on this problem instead of actually solving it, it would come back to bite me later on. Sort of like procrastinating on homework.

Soon, summer break would be over and the second semester would start. Most likely I'd spent the rest of the year in class instead of hiding in the gym loft...and if I had to guess, Adachi would too.

"*Nee-chan*, you're making a miso ocean."

"Huh?" At this, I looked down at my plate to find my cutlets drowning in a sauce swamp. "Whoa, whoa, whoa!" Hastily, I rescued each one, but it was too late. Their crispy batter had gone completely soggy.

"Ha ha!" My mother snickered like a little kid, pointing at me with her chopsticks and flicking globs of miso everywhere.

"Ugh. Remind me not to grow up to be like you."

"Please. You couldn't be like me if you tried."

I wasn't even annoyed—just baffled that we were fighting all of a sudden.

"That reminds me, Mom, how's your knee? You said it was hurting, right?" she asked Grandma, her chin sticky with miso. I hadn't heard anything about this, so I wasn't sure what exactly had reminded her.

Everyone looked at Grandma, who chewed her chicken and nodded. "All better now," she answered curtly.

"Really?"

"When you get to be my age, some part of your body's always in bad shape," she replied dismissively, like she was avoiding the subject.

At this, I looked over at Gon, his milky left eye staring into space from the corner of the kitchen. To me, it seemed like *every* part of him was in bad shape. Hopefully, he wasn't in pain though.

What did Gon seek from the world, now that his freedom was slowly being sapped away? Peace? Release? Or... something more optimistic?

"Blegh... Too salty." Unsurprisingly, the sauce overdose had rendered these cutlets well nigh inedible...and I still had a whole ocean of miso sauce left on my plate.

"Better eat it all up! Better not leave any! Better lick the plate if you have to!"

As it turned out, I didn't especially enjoy reaping what I'd sowed.

I set my new swimsuit and my cell phone side by side. Nope, this still didn't make much sense. I looked at each of them in turn. *Should I show Shimamura and ask her what she thinks? Seems stupid. Like, really stupid.* Fortunately, the fact that I realized this prior to taking action meant my brain was relatively functional today... and yet I still wanted to get her opinion.

Granted, I didn't have to ask her outright; I could always arrange an opportunity to wear it and find out then. *Should I invite her to something?* I bent forward, leaning close to the phone. Just because we already went to the pool once didn't mean we couldn't go back a second time. Or I could invite her somewhere else. I had no shortage of places I wanted to take her. A summer festival, the aquarium, the planetarium...

When my parents took me to these places, I learned a lot, but had trouble expressing my feelings. This time, however, I was confident I could be more open with my emotions. As long as I was with Shimamura, anywhere we went had value.

So let's call her, I told myself, spurring on my cold feet. If I kept hesitating, I'd miss another chance.

I still hadn't forgotten the night I saw her walk past. The memory made a dark heat well up in my eyes. That night at the summer festival, Shimamura was walking side by side with some other girl, smiling at her...

Who *was* she, anyway? I wanted to know, but I didn't want Shimamura to tell me. I didn't want to hear about her other friendships; the words would stab my eardrums like a hot poker, and I'd lose whatever composure was currently keeping my emotions safely beneath the water's surface. If I exploded at her like last time, she would probably cut ties with me for good...and that was the one thing I could not abide.

Thus, I needed to keep myself in check. But every time I thought about Shimamura or met up with her, I could feel the water levels rising, waves crashing like an unruly ocean, depicting the storm in my heart. I couldn't let myself lose control, and yet distancing myself wasn't the right answer either. But I lacked the experience to know how to gauge these things by sight alone. Objectively speaking, I was immature...and that immaturity was goading me onward to the day highlighted on my calendar.

Just three more days... What was Shimamura doing right now, all the way on the other end of the calendar? I wanted to hear her voice. I wanted to connect with her, if only over the phone. At least then I could be sure she was thinking about me.

Passion superseded fear, and I reached for my phone. But I didn't want to call her up out of the blue, so I decided to ask permission with a quick email:

"May I call you?"

...Seriously, why was I always so formal?

"Thing is, I'm over at my grandpa's house. In an even *smaller* town, if you can believe it."

"Ooh, gotcha. I forgot that's what you always do for the Bon Festival."

At long last, the sun had mercifully sunk beneath the horizon, leaving behind a night of chirping cicadas. I walked through the shadowy soundscape as I talked with Tarumi over the phone. She had invited me to hang out tomorrow, but obviously, I had to turn her down. This seemed to remind her of the past somehow.

"I feel like you used to bring me souvenirs too..."

"I did?"

"Uhhhh... Maybe not? Not like our prefecture's got any specialty products, I guess."

"Sure we do! We've got persimmons, and sweetfish, and...*kurikinton*...?" This prefecture was my home, but I only had an outsider's view of it.

I crouched down in front of the doghouse. Grandpa's house was small, and the walls were thin, so I had chosen to take the phone call outside. It really drove home just how useful cell phones could be... *Great, now I sound like an old person.*

"I swear, there's nothing good about our town... Shima-chan, haven't you ever thought about moving to the big city?"

"Hmmm..."

"You know, enroll at a college in Tokyo? Or even just a college in Nagoya!"

Judging from her tone and choice of words, Tarumi wanted to get away from the countryside. But...would a different city really be that much better?

Everybody always acted like big cities were inherently superior for some reason. Some of the older kids I used to play with went to Tokyo and never came back. Maybe Tarumi could see the same appeal they saw.

"No, I haven't thought about it. I don't even know if I'm going to college at all," I answered honestly.

"WHAT?!" came the startled reply. "Really? You're just gonna get a JOB?"

Her voice was louder now—was it really that hard to believe? I didn't have the motivation to study for four more years. My mom would just tell me not to go.

"Yeah, assuming I can find one, anyway. And I think I'd rather stay here."

Maybe I could work at a local bakery somewhere. I liked bread, and I had some connections... Granted, maybe it wasn't that simple. But I couldn't think of a job I actually *wanted*. I had no prospects.

It was too dark to see inside the doghouse. No one lived there anymore.

"Hmmm. Wow... Well, okay."

Her voice probed around me, like a wild animal tentatively approaching something it didn't under-stand. Once she identified me by scent, how would she react...? I decided to change the subject before I could find out.

"So was that your way of asking for a souvenir?"

"Huh? No, no, nothing like that. Not at all... But I

mean, hey, if you *did* want to get me something..." She trailed off, laughing. *Yep, she's totally trying to be slick.*

Casually, I put my hand in the doghouse. In the darkness, something felt off about the blanket I touched, so I grabbed it and pulled it out. I was expecting something stiff and scratchy, but instead it was soft. I brought it close to my face.

It was an old turquoise blanket I had bought long ago. But in contrast with the dirty doghouse, it was *clean*. Someone had washed this blanket and brought it back out here—back to a home that had lost its only resident.

For a moment, I couldn't speak. Reflexively, I searched for my grandmother beyond the darkness.

"Shima-chan?"

"Oh, uhh, it's nothing. If I see a cool souvenir, I'll get it for you," I blurted hastily.

"No, no, you don't have to! I mean...you know...it's not about the souvenir. It's about you," she blurted just as quickly.

"What do you mean?"

"Well...I want to see you again, that's all. You're all I really...*need*, I guess? Uhh, I think maybe I said too much. Yeah, definitely said too much!"

Half-listening to Tarumi's long, apologetic tangent, I returned the blanket to its proper place. Was this what it meant to "feel sentimental"? Cold air rushed into the empty hole in my chest, and it stung.

"I feel like I'm only gonna dig myself deeper, so uhhh, I think I'll run along now!" Tarumi announced cheerfully, though it sure didn't seem like something she was meant to be cheerful about.

"Not sure I get it, but okay."

"Let's meet up again when you're back in town, Shima-chan!"

"Okay!" And with that, I promptly ended the call.

Then, ten seconds later, I got an email from Adachi: *"May I call you?"*

"Gosh, I'm so popular," I joked to myself.

Adachi always asked permission first. While it *did* seem like it would be tiring to have to ask before every little phone call, I could appreciate the effort to be polite and considerate. It spoke volumes about her moral fiber.

"Yes, ma'am," I wrote back, and without missing a beat, my phone rang. It was kinda cute. I could picture her sitting cross-legged on her bed, waiting patiently.

"Hey hey!"

"Hello?"

Somehow, the order felt backward.

"Shimamura?"

"Hey heyyyy!" I repeated, louder and longer this time. I could hear the chirping of some insect I didn't recognize.

"Uhh...are you in a good mood or something?"

"Not really. I've just been talking for a while already, so I'm all warmed up, I guess? I was on the phone with another friend just now."

I decided to just be honest with her. Would she get upset again? To tell the truth, she could be a real hassle sometimes. Not that I was perfect at social stuff myself, but man, she was somehow even worse than me. She seemed *desperate* to make our friendship work, and I was a little bit curious to learn why...but I knew if I asked, things would probably get messy again. So instead I let it go. But maybe that was why she blew up last time—because I never gave her the opportunity to explain herself.

Our friendship was complicated, but perhaps that was to be expected when one of us was a total enigma.

"Hggghh..."

It was the sound of something being inhaled—Adachi was taking a deep breath, I guess. Kinda sounded like she was holding something back.

"So...h-how are you doing out there?" Her voice was hard, but she was making an effort to continue the conversation. It wasn't quite natural, but definitely an improvement.

"What do you mean?"

"Are you...reliving old memories, or...enjoying the fresh air, or something? I wouldn't know what it's like out there."

"Oh... Yeah, I've been thinking about the past, I guess," I lied. Then I ran from what was hiding on the other side of the lie. "How was your day today?"

"Mine? Well, uh, I went to work..."

"Ooh, how very responsible."

"And then on my way home I bought a swimsuit."

"A swimsuit? Don't you already have one?" I thought back to our trip to the pool and her classy little one-piece.

"I do, but um...I figured I should probably have an extra, just in case."

"Oh, interesting. Going to the beach or something?"

She was a little old to be going with her parents, though. Not that she would.

"Well, um...uhhhh...y-yeah, totally. With you."

"What? That's funny; I don't remember making plans to go to the beach."

"No, I was just...thinking it'd be cool to go with you sometime! How about it?!"

Her invitation was so aggressive, she practically bit my ear off. It really threw me for a loop. Her voice was all wavery and pitchy too... *Classic Adachi, I guess.*

"I mean, yeah, it'd be cool. But we're nowhere near the ocean."

"Uhhh...o-okay then, the river!"

"I don't know about that. It's dangerous to play in the river."

That was what a certain *someone* once told me after she slipped and cut her head open on a rock at the riverbed.

"Okay then, uhhh...a pond...?"

If I said no, I had the feeling she'd invite me to a swamp next. Apparently, she *really* wanted to go to a body of water somewhere. Heck, maybe she'd settle for a communal bathhouse if it meant she could show off her new swimsuit... Was it really *that* cute? Now I was curious.

"Hey, you should send me a picture."

"Wh-what? A picture of what?"

"Your swimsuit!" I teased.

"What for...?" she mumbled. But I could hear her voice grow distant, so clearly she had decided to oblige. *Well, that was easy.* Maybe she really *did* want to show off her cute swimsuit. I lowered my phone from my ear while I waited, and sure enough, I received an email a short while later with an image attached.

It was a photo of the swimsuit lying on her bed. Incidentally, it was my favorite shade of blue. *Hmmm. Not wrong, per se, but not what I wanted.*

"I want to see you *wearing* it, silly."

"Wh-wh-why, though? What for?"

"Try again, please."

I ignored her confusion and repeated my request. I didn't have an answer to her question; I just wanted to see her reaction, that's all. I didn't have a mirror on me, but I could feel myself smirking impishly. As I waited in silence like a total bully, I heard her move away from the phone.

She had decided to oblige, part two.

For some reason, I was really excited to see what she would send me...and sure enough, it met my every expectation.

"Ha ha!"

Her face was far more interesting than the swimsuit—she was trying to smile, but her embarrassment had clearly won out. Her lips were frozen in place, her bangs were sweaty and sticking to her forehead, and her eyes screamed, "Help me!" Her left arm was extended in the traditional selfie fashion, but because she was bent over, she kind of looked like she was doing a superhero pose. It was a still image, but I could practically see her trembling from head to toe.

"Ha ha ha ha! Thanks."

I could hear some kind of faint thumping sound on

the other end of the line, like she was punching a pillow or something.

"Pretty eye-catching, I gotta say."

More thumps. The thought that she was punching her pillow *in a swimsuit* was somehow even funnier.

"So where do you want to wear your new swimsuit? The beach? The river? The swamp?" I pressed mischievously.

Hesitantly, she answered: "...The bathhouse."

Wait, really? I pictured it and laughed. "Okay, then, let's go once I get back."

The communal bathhouse was *not* generally somewhere a couple of teen girls would hang out. But for a moment, I thought to myself: perhaps it was precisely that departure from social norms that kept me coming back to her.

After that, we chatted idly for a while longer. Oddly enough, the conversation was actually fun for a change. But eventually, I started getting thirsty, and when the chirping shifted from insects to birds, I decided to call it a night.

"Sleep well, Adachi." Surprisingly enough, my voice was soft and kind. So kind, in fact, it alarmed me.

"Oh, um...g-good night, Shimamura-san."

She addressed me formally for some reason. Reflexively, I bowed my head in return. Then I hung up the phone and let out a sigh.

So she bought a swimsuit, huh? I marveled at the steps she was taking to improve. All day long, I'd found myself thinking about Adachi here and there, but I certainly never anticipated *this*.

On the other end of the calendar, time was passing, and things were changing. Even when I wasn't looking, life went on—births, deaths, chance encounters. Somewhere in the world, someone was facing a big problem; somewhere in the world, windmills were turning; somewhere in the world, someone just bought a Coke from a vending machine; somewhere in the world, deep-sea creatures were thriving.

Changing, creating, filling, aging, withering, fading. But I didn't really understand all that. I was still every bit as innocent and ignorant as I was when I was a child.

I rested my arms on top of my bent knees and buried my face, listening to the faint sounds of my own breathing. But try as I might, I couldn't find the overlap between myself and the younger me who crouched in front of this same doghouse all those years ago. No matter how long I waited here, no tears would ever come.

Just then, I heard a noise and looked up. The pressure against my eyes had turned my vision fuzzy, blurring the already indistinct darkness.

I had received an email from Adachi. Once again, it was just a single heart emoji.

"Is this part of her routine now...?"

I debated whether to respond, but ultimately decided to send a heart back. *My heart is with you, Adachi!* I joked to myself, playfully clutching my chest. But I was already pretty heartless, so I couldn't afford to send much more.

I thought back to the ocean of miso at dinner. Life would probably be a lot more painful if my heart was all melty like that. But because I had avoided those sorts of confrontations, I was probably really fragile, actually. My heart and body were detached, and now I was incapable of detecting any changes.

I lowered my phone, gazed into the empty doghouse, and basked in the sleepy countryside. And as I listened to the whir of a bicycle in the distance, I thought back to the cityscape on my mother's old closet.

A (Failed) Visit to the Hino Estate

EVERY NOW AND THEN, I liked to show up at Hino's house unannounced so I could throttle her. Wait, throttle her? No, *startle* her? Same difference. I decided not to think too hard about it. Anyway, the goal was to make her scream.

As I entered the bamboo forest that led to her mansion, my whole environment shifted. The densely packed bamboo trees absorbed the bright sunshine, and the breeze that blew through the gaps was nice and cool, brushing against me gently. As I traveled down the cobblestone path, the sunlight filtered in through the gaps, creating a tranquil little pocket of space.

But as soon as the bamboo trees came to an end, so too did my peaceful moment away from the heat. What lay before me was a sprawling plot of land so lush and green, I half-expected to see turtles and cranes living in perfect harmony. Hino's house truly was a mansion; even at a distance, I could smell the high-quality wood. And apparently, it wasn't just her short stature that made it look big by comparison.

I could see an intercom at the front entrance, so I pressed it.

"Yes?" It was Hino's older brother, uh...Kotarou, I think?

"Greetings!"

"Oh, if it isn't Akira's schoolmate..." Apparently, he remembered me too.

"Meats, sir." *Wait, I said the wrong thing.* But I was already starting to sway, so it was too late to take it back.

"One moment, please." Then I heard him call down the hallway: "Akira! Your friend is here!"

"What?!" It was Hino, and she didn't sound happy.

"Your FRIEND! IS! HERE!"

"Woohoo, it's me!" I chimed in, just for fun.

"What friend?"

"Me, silly!"

"Oh. The heck are *you* doing here?"

"To hang out with you, duh!"

A few moments later, Hino came dashing out to the front. Sadly, she wasn't wearing a yukata, which was a shame, because she looked great in them.

"Oh, good grief. You totally forgot, didn't you?" Rolling her eyes, she scratched her forehead.

"No, I didn't. I made it here all by myself."

"Gee, I'm so proud."

"Hee hee hee hee hee..." I liked it when Hino gave me compliments. Hers were always my favorite.

"That was sarcasm, genius."

"Huhwha?!"

Then I caught a glimpse of Hino's mom rushing down the hall. She always wore kimonos, even on Bring Your Parents to School Day, so it made her really easy to find, though Hino seemed embarrassed about it for some reason.

"She sure seems like she's in a hurry."

I could see two carry-on suitcases sitting by the entryway...but then an assistant came and brought out a third one. Hino glanced over at them, then looked back at me. "Well, we're flying out to Hawaii today, remember?"

"You are?" *How much tanner are you trying to get?*

"I told you this was happening, like, a week ago."

"Sorry, I don't remember."

"Yeah, I'm not really surprised."

Yes, sometimes I forgot things about Hino, especially the things I didn't like. "How long will you be gone?"

"I already told you. Six days."

"Sorry, I don't—"

"It's fine! My point is, no, I can't hang out with you."

"Hmm. I see." Since it was hot, I stepped into the entryway and sat down to think it over. "You know, now that I think about it, you go abroad every year, don't you?"

"Something like that, yeah."

Belatedly, I remembered: this same thing had been happening since grade school. I could remember when she left for a trip last year, but absolutely nothing in between. Then she turned to look at me, so I greeted her with a bright smile. "Well, you can count on me to watch the house for you!"

"Go home!"

And just like that, she kicked me out. *Grrrr, she's so mean! Well, I guess she's busy... Wouldn't want to get in her way...* And so I reluctantly trudged home, making cicada sounds as I went. *Wait, do cicadas even like bamboo?* Curious, I looked up.

"Hey, Nagafuji!"

Just then, Hino came running after me. The shadows of the bamboo trees fell over her tanned skin, perfectly encapsulating the season of summer.

"Here." She tossed me something, and I caught it. It was a bottle of green tea, perfectly chilled. "I'll get in touch once I'm back from my trip, so...yeah, just come on over—no, actually, I'll go to you," she corrected herself hastily as she looked back over her shoulder at her house.

My house or her house? As long as she was there, it didn't really matter. "Just leave it to me, the Great Nagafuji!"

"Since when are you 'the Great Nagafuji'?" she sighed, laughing.

"Oh, and I want souvenirs."

"Yeah, I know. I'll buy you some cool snacks or something."

Somehow, she always knew just what I wanted. Then she ran off back to the house, and I watched her go. Before she disappeared, she turned and gave me a little wave, so I waved emphatically back at her. She scowled for a moment, then waved back just as hard as me. So I waved even harder! This time she ignored me and disappeared. *Grrrr.*

Anyway, so there I was, toddling home from Hino's place...

"Hmmm. Well, *now* what do I do?"

As I walked through the bamboo grove, I tried to think of somewhere else I could go but came up empty-handed. *Should I just go home and lounge around in front of the fan?* She would be gone for the next six days. How would I *survive*? My head was going to explode!

"Oh...?"

Just then, I recognized a head of shimmering blue hair coming my way. It was the same little girl who stopped by the shop every now and then. She was toddling along just like me, but when she noticed me, she stopped short to scrutinize me carefully.

"Ohhhhh!"

"Whoaaaa!"

In perfect sync, we both broke into a run and came crashing into each other.

Boom!

But despite her short stature, the little girl managed to stay upright. Impressive leg muscles on this one.

"You're the croquette lady, aren't you?"

"More or less," I answered.

"Shimamura-san and Little have gone out, so I no longer have any place to be."

"Yeah, and Hino's going on a trip...so *I* no longer have anything to entertain me."

We pulled each other into a tight embrace.

"Sniffle, sniffle!"

"Waaahhh!"

After a good long cry, we pulled apart. *Ugh, I'm so sweaty.* Not because of the little girl, but because I cried too hard. "So are you free right now?"

"Indeed I am," the girl smiled back. She wasn't sweating in the least, and her hair was dry and soft. She probably wasn't an android, and yet her hair color was far from natural. It was all very mysterious.

"Well, wanna come back to my place?"

"I happily accept your invitation."

She agreed readily, without thinking too hard. But I, on the other hand, had all sorts of thoughts. Thoughts like: *Heh heh heh, I'm going to make you work at the register so I don't have to!* She looked an awful lot like our mascot character anyway.

"Want some?"

I twisted the cap off the tea bottle and offered it to her. She jumped up to take it, and as she drank, I thought I could practically see the green liquid sliding down her ghostly pale throat.

And so I took my little stray home with me.

"Today I've found us the perfect poster girl," I announced to my mother when we got home. Her eyes widened.

"Why, it's the little errand girl!"

"Hello there, ma'am." Perfect manners, this one. Clearly, she was a good fit for customer service.

"Listen here, little blue girl. All you have to do is clap your hands and shout stuff like 'Yummy treats, on sale now!'"

"I beg your pardon?"

"It's super easy, trust me."

"And yet *you* still seem to struggle with it," my father remarked sarcastically from the back of the store. But I ignored him.

"Go on!"

I gave her little shoulders a push. She stood next to the display case and clapped her little hands. "Hey, hey, come on in!"

"Ooh, that's the spirit!"

"On sale! On sale now!"

She clapped and clapped while the mascot Hino drew for us hung just overhead. The more I compared the two, the more identical I found them. And now that I thought about it...it didn't really fit with the whole butcher theme at all.

"That reminds me, weren't you going to go stay the night over there?" Mom asked.

"Hino's family's leaving for Hawaii today," I answered, swinging the bag I'd packed. And boy, was I ever disappointed. Without Hino, my whole summer break would be totally lopsided. *Am I using that word right? Eh, who cares.*

As the little blue girl clapped her hands, she looked up at me, her coach. "You and Hino-san are very close friends, aren't you, Nagafuji-san?"

"You could say that," I nodded as I leaned against the display case. *Wait, when did she learn our names?*

"Well, *I'm* very close with Shimamura-san and Little," she declared proudly, her hair sparkling even in the absence of any sunlight. Apparently, she felt like bragging.

"Wow."

I didn't know who "Little" was supposed to be, but it wasn't easy to get close to Shimamura. While at first glance she seemed friendly, she never got too invested. She probably wasn't that attached to me or Hino either.

"For the record, I'm Hino's best friend," I told her, just to make sure there was no room for doubt, but now that I thought about it... "Hmmmm..."

If being Hino's best friend was my most notable trait, then maybe I could work as her assistant in the future. That wouldn't be the worst. Maybe she could pull some strings and get me hired without an interview... Actually, more than likely, she'd be passionately opposed to it. You know, sometimes I really didn't understand the way her brain worked.

After that, the little blue girl worked as our mascot until evening. Apparently, her striking blue hair helped draw customers in—middle-aged ladies would stop dead in their tracks to stare at her, and then I'd pull them into the store. Sure enough, I had an eye for true talent!

Oh, and I gave her some tips about how to interact with friends too.

Then we had dinner together, we took a lukewarm bath together, and she went home for the night. I didn't know where her home was, but her little blue sparkles floated around the store for quite some time after she left.

I sat cross-legged in the center of the room, wearing my swimsuit. Every time I tried to open my mouth, sweat trickled down my back. Clutching my head, I curled into a ball on the floor and writhed in shame and regret.

WHY did you want a picture of me in my swimsuit, Shimamura?! And god, why did I look so awkward?! Kill me!!!

Flailing and rubbing my forehead against the carpet, I agonized over my expression, trying to think of some way I could have looked a little less stupid.

3. The Hometown Dog

IN THE BEGINNING, I didn't want to go. For one thing, I barely knew my grandparents, and for another, I sincerely despised the thought of spending three whole days bored out of my skull without my friends or comic books. But my parents paid no mind to the sullen look that was (probably) on my little face at the time, and since the grown-ups were in charge, I was dragged out to the countryside regardless.

When I arrived, however, I quickly changed my tune. The instant I laid eyes on that fuzzball, the dull, empty scenery lit up in dazzling colors; when I reached out, he jumped at me eagerly. We were both too young to be mistrusting, and so we quickly became each other's only playmate. His name was Gon, and he was the new puppy my grandparents had just adopted.

In a blink, the two of us were already licking each other's cheeks and noses—okay, maybe the licking was a little more one-sided. From Gon's perspective, everyone else was huge, so for all I knew, maybe he targeted me as the weakest-looking of the bunch. Likewise, from my perspective, he was easier to hug and hold than the much bigger dog behind him. He was tiny, with fuzzy baby fur, and I could pick him up with one hand. Naturally, I took a liking to him right away.

No matter where I went, Gon was right there with me—the only exception was the bathtub. He would even sleep in my bed with me, but I could never get much sleep myself since I was terrified of rolling over and crushing him by accident. Ultimately, I ended up sleeping right up against the wall. That was how I discovered neck cramps for the first time in my young life.

Point being, Gon was my best friend for those three days I spent trapped out here. By the end, I was so infatuated with him that when it came time for us to go back home, I cried and threw a tantrum because I didn't want to be apart from him. Looking back, that was the first time I ever threw a fit...and it was probably the last time too. My parents weren't sure how to console me, so they offered to let me adopt my own puppy back home, but I didn't want a different puppy—I wanted *Gon*.

My grandma understood the problem faster than anyone else. I could remember her flicking my mother on the forehead to rebuke her. Then she turned and scolded me quietly: "No tantrums." With one sentence, she put an end to my tears, then stroked my hair and added, "There will always be next year."

Her touch was so gentle, it reminded me of how much I'd complained on my way here. I was sure I didn't deserve her kindness, and so I started crying all over again, this time for a different reason. Choking through my tears, I promised her and Grandpa that I'd come back.

Sniffling, I gave Gon one last hug, and he happily nuzzled his face against mine. I prayed I would remember his warmth forever... I never wanted to forget, no matter how much time passed.

I wanted to remember him, if only in my dreams.

And so I dreamed of my past. Cliché, I know. For some reason I was watching from a third-person perspective, and truth be told, I couldn't bear to watch myself cry openly, even as a child. Feelings of shame and something akin to guilt filled my chest, scorching my cheeks.

I could feel sweat clinging to my back, my forehead, and my nose. Slowly, I opened my eyes. My consciousness felt like it was being squeezed out of a tube, scattering in the wind, and everything was fuzzy still. My head ached as I looked over at the window. Through the gaps in the curtains, I could see the faint beginnings of dawn.

My sister was curled up in a ball in the bed with me, sleeping as soundly as a cicada. Taking care not to rustle the light summer blanket, I eased myself to my feet, then crept from the room and down the stairs so I wouldn't wake her. For once, I wasn't feeling like a sleepy little sloth today. But there was a different sort of fog in my mind, and I wanted to get some fresh air to clear it away.

"Itchy..."

I scratched my elbow. The mosquitoes had devoured me mercilessly last night, paying no mind to my nostalgic, sentimental mood. They weren't so easygoing as to let a free meal slip away from them.

Down on the first floor, all was dark and quiet. Apparently, no one else was awake yet. Keeping my distance from the bedrooms, I walked around to the living room, where I found Gon lying next to the TV. Despite the summer heat, he was all wrapped up in a blanket, unmoving. Anxiously, I crouched down, reached out to touch his muzzle, and was relieved to confirm that he was still breathing. His face was perfectly relaxed; I could only hope he was resting comfortably, unrestrained by the burden of his heavy body.

As I gazed at him, my lips parted. I wanted to tell him something, but the words wouldn't come. How could I begin to express the way I felt? I couldn't find the answer. It was like I had turned into Adachi: all emotion and zero communication.

In the end, I walked away without saying a word. Like a coward, I headed to the back door, slipped on my sandals, and fled the house. I didn't lock the door behind me, but I wasn't planning to go far, so I figured it was no big deal. Not like any burglars were awake at this hour anyway, right? Belatedly, I let out a yawn.

Even the cicadas were still sleeping; the only sound was the rhythmic crunch of gravel under my feet as I walked down the driveway. Dawn was fast approaching, but the darkness of night still lingered in the sky. The air wasn't especially cold either—just the lukewarm leftovers from yesterday's sunshine. It matched my dull gray surroundings to a T. But this color scheme was a familiar one.

Every year, summer break would roll around, and for three days I'd struggle to sleep in a bed that wasn't mine. I'd end up waking up ahead of everyone else in the house, so I'd go outside to entertain myself without disturbing anybody, and like clockwork, Gon would pick up my scent and chase after me. We spent so many hours just running around the driveway together... This was back when my sister was still in diapers.

The one thing I could remember more clearly than anything else was the feeling of Gon's face nuzzled against mine. He was so big and fluffy, it felt like I was hugging a cloud. Those were some of the happiest moments of my entire life.

Gon and I were both so innocent—so *ignorant*. We never stopped to think about what lay ahead. I saw him every year, so while leaving him never got any easier, I believed beyond a shadow of a doubt that we would always have more time to run around together. And now those same feelings were killing me inside. I was so relieved that he was alive, but at the same time, it hurt.

"I like you" wasn't enough, but "I love you" didn't feel right. It was (hopefully) too early for "Thanks for everything," but "Be well" didn't seem to fit either. So what exactly did I want to tell him? How did I want to unchain myself from this misery that filled my chest, my throat, and now my mind?

I stared down at my feet, but found no kernels of wisdom. Frustrated, I ran my hands through my unbrushed hair. I knew something was lurking in me, deep down, making me restless. But...I...

"Oh, hello. Bit early to go for a walk, isn't it?"

I flinched at the sudden voice. *That would make two of us, sir.*

It was the neighbor, Iwaya-san. Like yesterday, he was wearing a turban, but today he had a large backpack over his shoulders. With his wrinkles and his tanned skin, he looked like a traveling sage from a distant land. Not exactly the kind of next-door neighbor you'd usually see out here in the sticks. I wasn't expecting to encounter anyone outside, except maybe the newspaper delivery guy—so what was he doing, wandering onto our private property and striking up casual conversations like he owned the place?

"Good morning," I replied stiffly.

"Yes, good morning," he replied without batting an eye. "Then again, there aren't many people outside at this time of day, so it makes for a rather peaceful stroll."

"Oh, uh...yeah...I guess so." Truth be told, this countryside village was so small, I was having trouble believing it ever *wasn't* peaceful.

"So you're...uhh, hmmm. The granddaughter?"

"I'm Shimamura. Shimamura Hougetsu."

"Ah, just like the famous literary critic! Well, that'll be easy to remember!"

He let out a hearty laugh, and the sight of his smile reminded me: There used to be an older girl who would arrive to visit family around the same time as me, come to think of it. Whenever we were both in town, the two of us would always play together with Gon. Judging from the age difference, that girl was probably Iwaya-san's granddaughter.

All that aside, I was distracted by the object in his hands. When he noticed me looking, he extended his arm and thrust it in my face. "This what you're lookin' at?" It was a small, crudely made bowl.

"Uh, yeah," I answered vaguely. After all, it wasn't the sort of thing someone generally carried around outside. At my response, however, he gleefully held it aloft.

"Well, you see, my granddaughter made it for me!"

"Huh?"

"She's training to be a ceramic artist, and she recently made me this bowl. My very own custom bowl!"

"Oh... Cool..."

Now I understood why he was carrying it around—so he could brag to someone. Who did he expect to find wandering around at dawn before even the cicadas were awake? I got the sense that everyone who knew this eccentric old man was worried about him, and for a variety of reasons.

"Doesn't it just speak to you? Can you feel the intellectual depth of the plain design?"

"Ha ha... Sad to say, I don't know too much about the fine arts," I replied with an awkward smile.

"Not to worry! My granddaughter's masterpiece resonates with even the most ignorant of children!"

"Ha ha." I wasn't mad, but I sure wasn't smiling anymore.

"Therefore, I shall bestow unto you this fishing pole."

"What do you mean, *therefore*...?"

The locals here (my mother included) didn't seem to understand how to connect their sentences correctly. But sure enough, he offered me a fishing pole. Reluctantly, I took it, though I wasn't sure what need I would have of it. It was a plain black pole—actually, I felt like I recognized it from somewhere. *There aren't any flea markets around here, are there?*

"Go rediscover your inner child and fish to your heart's content."

"How are those two things related...?" Actually, I hadn't gone fishing since the time I went with Hino last year.

"Not to worry! Once you're done, you can just give it back to your grandpa for me."

"Oh, so *that's* why."

"When you need to think for a while, fishing's your best bet."

I looked up sharply. *Did he read my mind?*

"After all, if you just sit around, you're liable to fall asleep!" he continued, his bushy beard puffing up like a cloud with each word.

"Ugh, yeah. Relatable." Every time I folded my arms to mull something over, I'd find myself lying in bed five minutes later.

"Oh?"

Just then, Iwaya-san craned his neck to look behind me. Then I heard a scratching sound at the back door and turned to look. Judging from the size of the silhouette and the big ears, I had a feeling I knew who it was... I raced over and opened the door, and sure enough, Gon looked up at me with sleepy eyes.

"Aww, Gon..." *Did I wake you on my way out? Poor guy.*

In the past he would eagerly follow me outside, but today he didn't even jump up at me. With his cloudy left eye, he was a shadow of his former self. And at some point, I grew tall enough to tower over him, my shadow engulfing him completely...

I felt a stinging pain in my nose, like I'd popped a blood vessel. I felt compelled to reach up and pinch it shut, lest blood start trickling down. It was already feeling wet in there as it was... Probably just sweat or something, though.

Looking at Gon made me feel a lot of different ways. But for once in my life, I couldn't find the words to describe it, and no amount of thinking could help me. So instead I crouched down and stroked his head.

"Good morning, Gon."

It's important to start the day by saying hello, I reassured myself quietly. He barked back in response. But if I didn't find a solution to this communication breakdown, I was no better than Adachi.

"Oh, if it isn't Gon! Didn't know you were still alive, old boy. Guess we're both too stubborn to kick the bucket, eh?"

Iwaya-san held out his hand for Gon to shake, but the dog didn't move. Then Iwaya-san reached out and grabbed a paw for himself. Gon didn't object. After a small handshake, the old man let go.

"Then again, I was already one foot in the grave when you got here, wasn't I?" He let out a hearty chuckle. "Well, I'll be seeing you."

Time froze as the old man locked eyes with the old dog. It felt a bit too long and drawn-out to be a simple morning greeting. But after it was over, Iwaya-san turned and walked away. He was still so full of energy... On reflex, I called out to him.

"Hey, um..."

"What is it, child?" the man asked in a kindly voice. And as it turned out, with a little encouragement, even the heaviest of questions could tumble off my tongue.

"Does getting older make life harder?"

There was nothing to be gained from asking him this question, and yet I didn't think twice about it.

"Hmmm." His turban swayed with the motions of his head as he mulled it over. "I should have known a literary girl like you would ask deep, esoteric questions."

"I'm not a literary girl," I retorted before I could stop myself. If anyone was "esoteric" here, it was him.

"I've got a granddaughter who sends me handmade pottery, so I can't say my life's very hard at all. Does that answer your question?" he asked, his eyes gleaming.

"Yes, of course." *Not at all, actually. Clearly, I asked the wrong person.*

"Next time, I suggest you reserve that sort of question for someone whose answer you truly wish to hear." He shot a pointed look at Gon, then bounced on his heels, adjusting his grip on his backpack. "Now then, I've got another day of treasure-hunting ahead of me!"

"Treasure-hunting?"

"If I got my way, I'd be searching the ocean floor right about now..."

And so he walked off, grumbling to himself as he went. Every time his turban bounced, I caught a glimpse of the sunrise on the horizon beyond him; I cast the fishing line in the direction of the light like I was trying to reel in the sun. *What if I could turn back time?* It was a stupid hypothetical, and yet I paused to consider.

"*Ask the dog*, he says. Would you even understand a word I said?" I asked Gon, tilting my head at him.

He simply stared back at me, squinting.

"Are you sure you can manage on your own, Hougetsu? Want me to come with you?" my grandmother asked fretfully when I told her I was going fishing.

Relax, Grandma. I'm not gonna fall and cut my head open like you *did.* "No, that's okay. I know you've got bad knees and all."

"Hi-*yah*!"

With a loud cry and surprisingly good form, she threw out a karate kick, her toes taut. Her leg went a lot higher than I expected too. But then she hunched over, clutching her foot.

"Grandma?!"

"Got a cramp in the arch of my foot..."

"Right. You sure are my mother's mother." *I can see the familial resemblance.*

"Okay, all better now! Let's see... What'll you do for lunch?"

"Not sure... I'm not planning to be gone for too long, though." I looked at the clock. Not even a full hour had passed since I ate breakfast, so lunchtime was still a good three hours from now.

"Let's pack you a lunch just in case. I'll make you some rice balls."

"Thanks, Grandma."

She jogged off into the kitchen and started prepping my food: rice balls with pork cutlets. "I'll put it in a lunch bag for you along with a water canteen. That ought to tide you over until lunch."

"Don't worry. I'll be sure to stay out of the sun." As I took the lunch bag, a shadow moved in my peripheral vision; I looked over and found Gon's cataracts looking back at me. "Gon!"

He walked over and rubbed his nose against my legs, tickling me.

"What's the matter, boy?" I asked, rubbing his back.

Grandma peeked in at us to check on Gon for herself,

then smiled warmly. "He wants to go with you," she explained on his behalf.

Well, he shouldn't. But I held my tongue.

"You know how he is. He always loves to follow you around."

"Yeah…"

But how long was that "always" going to last?

Would he even be able to walk that far?

In the past, the roads seemed to stretch on forever. But back in those days, we both had boundless energy. Now it felt like the opposite… Was it because we were bigger?

As I looked down at the dog, Grandma tore up some bread and put it in a little baggie. "Here's a snack for Gon."

"Thanks."

"If you get hungry, you can have some too."

"Um…c-cool."

"Oh, good gracious. I'm *joking*, dear!" She laughed merrily. Belatedly, I smiled. But then her expression went dead serious. "I'm *not* going senile," she insisted, her eyes wide and bloodshot.

Uh, Grandma, you're starting to freak me out.

On my way to the front door, I bumped into my sister, who had just finished brushing her teeth. The sides of her face were still damp too. *I swear, it's like she doesn't know how to use a towel.*

"Nee-chan, where are you going?"

"See that? Take a guess." I pointed to the fishing pole resting against the wall. My sister turned and looked at it.

"River fishing?" she murmured. "I'll come too."

"No can do, kiddo. It's too dangerous."

I held a hand up to stop her; naturally, she scowled. But I refused to take my sister to a place where she might get hurt. Call it my *sisterly instinct* or something.

"Then how come *Gon* gets to go?"

"Are you kidding me? He's *way* older than you."

He and I were only one or two years apart. We were practically the same age...and yet...I couldn't help but curse Mother Nature for how she designed his life cycle.

"Settle down, dear. Old Granny will play with you."

As my sister pouted, Grandma put a hand on her shoulder. Then my sister's frown faded, and she cocked her head. "You will?"

"We can play *Bomberman*!" Grandma exclaimed, ushering my sister along. *She just wants an excuse to play video games, doesn't she?* I thought to myself with an amused smirk.

I used to play video games with that neighbor girl too. But these days, she was learning how to make weird-looking bowls, apparently... Looking back, she was always good with her hands; she would fold origami animals for me. One time, we made a big ship out of newspaper.

"Oh, and Hougetsu, make sure to wear a hat while you're out."

Before she dragged my sister away, Grandma opened the shoe cupboard and pulled out a paint-splattered dark-blue baseball cap, which she then placed on my head. It smelled weather-beaten.

"What else... Oh, a parasol! You'll need one of those!"

Next, she pulled out a black umbrella and handed it to me. It was elegant and lacy, so it was probably hers. But with this in addition to the lunch bag and the fishing pole, I was starting to feel like a pack mule. Still, I couldn't possibly turn her down, so I let her fuss over me.

"Be careful out there, won't you?"

"I will. And when I come home, maybe we can all play together," I called out like a good big sister.

"No thanks," my sister shot back in a huff.

"Okay, then." *Man, she's such a brat. If only she took a leaf out of Yashiro's book and—actually, never mind. Bad idea.*

I locked the door behind me, then let out a warm sigh.

"Why is she so nice to me?"

How could *anyone* manage to be that kind-hearted? It was a mystery to someone like me, who always felt uncomfortable on the receiving end of someone else's goodwill.

"...Let's go, Gon."

And so off we went. Gon was already panting in the heat, but he trudged forward nonetheless. When I opened the umbrella, he moved close to my feet so he could be in the shade. If I started running, he probably wouldn't be able to keep up... It used to be the other way around, but now our roles were reversed.

Today, it felt like the cicadas' drone was an invisible net surrounding us. It was so perfectly rhythmic, it threatened to lull me to sleep if I listened for too long, so I shook it out of my mind and faced forward.

In the driveway, my father was holding the garden hose, washing the car. Probably easier to do it here than back home in our tiny driveway, I guess. He had his back turned, but he must have seen us coming in the car's reflection, because he turned to look at us—very nearly spraying me with water in the process.

"Heading out?"

"Yeah."

My father looked at Gon, then the fishing pole. "Haven't had a good carp dinner in a while."

"I'm not a miracle worker, Dad."

"Want me to drive you?" he offered, jerking his chin at the freshly cleaned car.

I looked down at Gon, then looked up. Beyond the

parasol lay a blue sky devoid of clouds. Then I slowly shook my head. "That's okay. We'll walk."

"Okie-doke. Be careful out there, pumpkin."

With that, my father went back to washing the car. He was already dripping with sweat, which made me wonder why he didn't turn the hose on himself instead.

Then Grandpa popped out from the house. "Wash ours too while you're at it, won't you, son?" he asked with a grin.

After that, Gon and I headed down the road the way my family had come when we first drove here, crossing over the little bridge and snaking our way down the hill to the riverside. Then the road looped back under the bridge in the direction of the mountains. It felt like I was traveling a secret path far removed from civilization, which gave me a little thrill.

When I was younger, I used to sneak away with Gon without telling anyone. Then one time, when Grandma came to find me, she slipped and cracked her head open. I could remember it all like it was yesterday. At the time, she had laughed it off, so I wasn't too worried about the blood loss, but looking back, it was a really serious injury.

Years later, when I was older, I realized it was indirectly my fault for going off to play at the river. That was the moment I first learned what guilt felt like, and I still regretted it to this day.

I wasn't really a...*considerate* sort of person, for lack of a better word. I was no pure-hearted saint. As a result, I hated feeling indebted to anyone, because that would mean I owed them kindness in return. But it was wrong to perform kindness purely out of obligation—at that point, it wasn't truly *kindness* anymore. I stumbled over this paradox over and over until eventually it began to affect my well-being. I knew maintaining strong interpersonal relationships was an important part of living a good life, but if it kept causing problems every time...

Blegh, I can't describe it. You can tell I don't use my brain too much.

"Now I'm confused..."

My vision began to spin like I was overheated. I put a hand over half of my face and waited for it to pass. When I looked down, Gon was sitting there, waiting patiently— no, he was probably exhausted himself, come to think of it. I crouched down beside him, stroked his head, and decided we'd take a break for a little longer. With the help of Grandma's parasol, the summer sun really wasn't too bad.

As I gazed down at Gon, his eyelids drooped like he was ready to take a nap, right there on the spot.

Then an intrusive thought barged in: If I ran off and left him here, what would happen to him? He didn't have the energy to chase after me anymore. Would he make it home hours later, hunt me down, and bite me? Or would he run out of energy, pass out on the side of the road, wither up, and...

The thought made me sick.

Sweat rose up from God knows where on me and dripped onto Gon, who flinched and moved away.

"Hey, it's not that gross! ...Okay, maybe it is."

I let out a dry laugh. He was slow in all things, even dodging my sweat drops. I stared down at him for a while, humming loudly for no clear reason.

"Okay, break time's over!" I announced as I straightened up. He didn't answer.

I wasn't confident I could shrug my shoulders and claim that this was simply the kind of person I was. Did I really know that for sure? It was all so *frustrating*.

We walked along the river shoreline, and as the buildings receded into the distance, the ground beneath my feet grew rocky and uneven. The road widened, and nature began to surround me on all sides—almost as if we were going back in time. The smell of dirt shifted to the smell of water. As the cicadas grew louder, the sound of cars in the distance began to fade. The babble of the brook was now close at hand; I could practically feel it washing me clean.

Overhead, the tree branches formed a lazy archway, serving as a protective roof. As we walked under it, the lush summery green seeped into us, and with each uneven step, my viewpoint shifted a tiny bit higher. Every lungful of fresh nature made me feel like something might take root inside me too.

A large, flat rock jutted out at a right angle over the river; I sat there to cast my line. At first I kicked back to relax, but over time I gradually hunched forward. The rock was in a shady spot, and yet somehow it had still absorbed the sun's heat, warming my butt through my shorts. The breeze felt nice, so I took off my baseball cap and let my long hair fly free, dancing in the wind. The air was cold enough to send a shiver down my spine, even in the middle of summer.

Gon lay in the shade of the parasol with his eyes closed. His perfect stillness against the flat rock made me anxious, so I reached out to pet him now and then. It was a relief to feel him breathing, however faintly. He opened his right eye to look at me, so I gave him some more pets before pulling my hand away. Then he closed his eye again.

According to Grandma, he would often sleep all day long. Did he spend his days drifting in and out of dreams? Was the Gon I saw before me merely sleepwalking?

But right as I settled in, I discovered a critical flaw in my plan:

"Wait... I forgot to bring a bucket for the fish..."

I wasn't the kind of wild child who could happily carry a flopping fish in her bare hands, so my father would just have to live without carp for another night. Not that I actually thought I could catch one, of course. Without any bait on the hook, I couldn't even lure in Yashiro.

When you need to think for a while, fishing's your best bet, or so I was told. But...did I have anything to think about?

"Hmmm..."

For some reason, Adachi came to mind. Maybe I saw a common thread between her and the dog sleeping wearily beside me. She always looked so defeated whenever things didn't go her way... She was the kind of girl who wore her heart on her sleeve, which I could appreciate. It really helped me understand her.

If I were to sum it up, Adachi just...didn't have much experience dealing with people. But that was exactly what made her so interesting to me. Speaking as someone whose overexposure to social interaction had left me numb to it, she was my polar opposite...and every now and then, I found myself tempted to protect her the way I wished someone would have protected me.

This was why I gently suggested that she try to make friends with other people. To me, this was hardly unreasonable...and yet I got the sense that Adachi would never truly fit in, no matter who told her to. School never taught us how to manage our emotions, and she had already spent her most formative years closed off to the world, so she was off to an extremely late start. She had skipped over all the simple stuff, so she was easily influenced by the strong personalities of everyone around her... *Right, that would explain why she's so unstable. That's why she latched onto me, and that's why I affect her so strongly.* I nodded to myself as the faint breeze stroked my cheek. Honestly, I half-expected her to profess her love for me any day now.

Then, as if Adachi had read my mind, my phone chose that exact moment to start ringing. I pulled it out of my bag and checked the screen.

"Oh, I was wrong."

It wasn't Adachi—it was Tarumi. I started to answer the phone, but my fingers froze. I looked at Gon. Our eyes met, and my throat quavered.

The phone rang loudly in protest, cutting in front of the cicadas. And as their drone receded into the background, it felt like those pests were looking down at us from a distance. Engulfed in noise, the back of my skull felt obnoxiously heavy. The phone was ringing...and I was just watching it ring.

In the end, I didn't pick up; I just held the phone and waited for it to stop. When it did, I promptly powered it off and tossed it back into my bag. Why on earth did I bring my phone out here? Nothing in the world was more nerve-wracking than letting a phone ring. It gave me anxiety like nobody's business.

But to be fair, this was possibly... *No, I shouldn't dance around it. Let's face it: This is my last chance to spend time with Gon.* But I could feel something—my conscience?— telling me I was just reaching for an excuse.

"What do you think?" I asked Gon as he lay beside me. He didn't seem to understand the question, and so he remained silent.

In the past, whenever our eyes met, he would jump up at me in joy, and we would do a gleeful little dance...but now neither of us moved a muscle. We used to run at full speed and feel the wind against our faces, but now we were strangers to it.

Shivering in the leisurely breeze, I directed my gaze into the distance.

"We've really grown up, haven't we?"

The words made my chest feel tight...and my throat... and my cheeks. Something swelled up inside me, wringing the breath from my lungs and circling around my eyes. What was this feeling? I couldn't remember. Did I always stiffen up like this whenever something happened to me?

But the river paid me no mind. It drifted along quietly, solemnly. The sky and earth didn't care one whit about the lives of those trapped between, and at this point, their apathy was starting to feel hostile.

I had no special powers. I couldn't keep Gon from dying. Here in reality, all his dozens of dreams would only melt away in the summer sun. What would be left of the time we shared after that? Would the sun shine down into his dreams?

As I sat there, holding the fishing pole with the cold wind blowing in my face, I thought long and hard.

With no fish to bring back for dinner, the two of us headed home empty-handed. Partway through, Gon's footsteps turned slow and deliberate, so I decided to make a pit stop on the side of the road. There, we sat and had ourselves a little picnic; Gon ate bread crumbs out of my hand like a large, ungainly bird. It reminded me of younger days when he used to beg me for food, and I averted my eyes.

Slowly, we traveled against the current of the river until we reached Grandpa and Grandma's house. As we walked up the driveway, I could see that my father had moved on to helping Grandpa polish *his* car. It certainly saved me the effort of having to go look for him later.

"Here you go, Grandpa."

"Welcome home, child. What's that you've got there?" He tilted his head in confusion, sponge in one hand, sweating profusely.

What the? "Uh...the neighbor said to return it to you..."

"Did I loan it out again? I don't remember, but my memory's not as good as his... Well, thank you, sweetheart." He took the fishing pole.

Then I sensed my father's gaze and raised my empty hands. "I don't have a carp for you, Dad."

"Darn it." He shook his head and lamented my failure. *You know, sometimes I really can't tell if you're joking or not.*

As I headed for the back door, I glanced at the doghouse. Unlike me, however, Gon showed absolutely no interest in it. It wasn't his—it belonged to the dog who preceded him. What sort of relationship did the two of them have? Whenever he saw the doghouse, did he think about his old friend? Or had he forgotten the other dog completely?

My shoulders ached as I opened the door. Inside, the first thing I heard was a shrill cackle.

"Eeee hee hee! Like taking candy from a baby!" Grandma declared as she sat in front of the living room TV.

"Grrrrr! I can't win at all!" my sister grumbled next to her, plainly pouting. Apparently. the old woman hadn't gone easy on her.

"I'm back."

"Oh, Hougetsu! Welcome home! Hee hee hee..." Grandma looked over her shoulder at me. She was still holding her controller and cackling. *Calm down, Grandma.*

As I was taking my shoes off, Gon walked into the house and heaved a breath, staring at the floor, tail hanging low. He looked utterly drained. "Get some rest, boy," I told him gently. He trudged over to the corner of the room, curled up under his blanket, and flopped down on the floor. I had bought him that blanket a long time ago, and frankly, I was impressed it was still in good condition.

Then I sat down next to my little sister, who smacked my head. Before I could even react, she leaned against me wordlessly, wriggling between my legs.

"What's wrong? Is somebody being a needy little baby?"

"Shut up!"

Why was she mad at me? As I grimaced, Grandma started laughing again. "Ho ho ho! Everybody loves Hougetsu."

"I wouldn't say *everybody*—"

"No, I don't!" my sister shot back. I tucked her hair behind her ear...and then I yanked on it. "Gyah!"

"Did you eat your lunch?" Grandma asked as she pressed buttons on the controller.

"Yup."

"If you're still hungry, I could warm up some more cutlets."

"Hmm..." I rubbed my tummy through my shirt. "Nah, I'm okay."

"All right then. If you get hungry, let me know. I got us some *kusa-dango* as a snack."

"Thanks." I let go of my sister's ear.

"What was *that* for?!" she protested. I smothered her face in my chest. "Mmffgg!"

My grandmother's words and deeds were brimming with love, which I interpreted as kindness. But I couldn't help but wonder: *Why*?

"Hey, Grandma?"

"What is it, sweetheart?"

"How can I learn to be kind, like you?"

A cartoon bomb exploded on the screen. She looked over her shoulder at me as she played. "What's wrong, Hougetsu?"

"Oh, no, it's nothing..." When she confronted me about my question head-on, it made me feel awkward for asking in the first place.

"Treat each day together like it's your last. With that mindset, you'll never take anyone for granted," she answered matter-of-factly, without a trace of pride, like it was the most obvious thing in the world. It was the kind of sentiment that spoke volumes about her character: open-hearted and generous.

In our culture, there's a saying: *Treasure every encounter, for it will never recur.* Rationally, I could see the logic in it right away; it was the sort of attitude I should have taken with Gon. But I couldn't picture myself actually taking this lesson to heart. I just couldn't give that much of myself for very long or else I couldn't survive in this world.

I hung my head, and my gaze drooped down to the dozing dog.

"You don't have to worry, dear. You're already a kind-hearted person."

I looked back at her and shook my head. "No, I'm really not." Was she just saying it to be nice? Even *I* could tell I wasn't the considerate type. I was missing that soft, gentle quality that actual kind people had.

Then she whirled around to face me and said, "Hougetsu, you're a real perfectionist, you know that?"

"...I am?" No one had ever said that to me before, and I wasn't sure how to react.

"You don't have to live your whole life in symmetry with everyone around you."

"...*What*?" *But that's the thing, Grandma—I'm not symmetrical with them at all.* "You know they were calling me a delinquent just last year, right?"

"Relax. When you were little, you were a good kid."

"And now...?"

"You're a *very* good kid!"

She reached out and stroked—no, *ruffled* my hair. My head bobbled around until my vision started to spin.

"You try too hard to keep your relationships perfectly even. When there's an imbalance, you start feeling uncomfortable. Frankly, you're so sincere, it's hard to believe you're related to my daughter at all!"

Setting aside the casual diss toward my mother—*me, sincere?* I thought back to how I handled the phone call at the river and found myself perplexed.

"I don't really get it," I replied, like the ignorant child I was.

But Grandma was a very patient woman. "Give me your number, Hougetsu."

"Huh?"

"Your phone number. I'll take photos of Gon and send them to you." She grinned at me, her face as round and soft as a *kusa-dango*.

At the sound of his name, I looked over at the dog. Surely she shouldn't have been able to connect the dots from my question alone... I was embarrassed that she could see through me so easily.

"Grandma, you have a cell phone?" my sister asked curiously, ignoring my angst.

"A *smartphone*, in fact!" Cackling, she pulled it out of her pocket and held it up like a 19th-century samurai pillbox. *Okay, maybe that analogy's a little too obscure.*

"Lucky!"

"If your parents get you a phone someday, do trade numbers with your old granny, won't you, dear?" Grandma grinned.

"Okay!" my sister nodded eagerly.

"And don't forget to give me your number later, Hougetsu." She shot me a thumbs-up, and I felt the will to resist drain from my body.

"Yaaaay..."

After that, I went limp until I could no longer feel the

fatigue from all that walking. Then Grandma put her phone away and picked up a controller instead. "Play with us, Hougetsu!"

"Sure, but...there's only two controllers..."

"Ever heard of a multitap?"

She opened the cabinet under the TV and pulled out an extender that added more controller ports. Once it was all plugged in, my sister sat up and grabbed her controller.

"You're being really mature today," I praised her, since she hadn't interrupted my conversation with Grandma. Then she stuck her tongue out at me. *I stand corrected.* Why did she always have to pick a fight with me over every little thing?

Just then, the bedroom door opened and my mother walked out, rubbing her eyes. With a big yawn, she sat down next to us.

"Finally awake, are you?"

"Yep..."

She had a gnarly case of bedhead, particularly in the back, where it stuck up in all directions like a lion's mane. This was one trait I wished I hadn't inherited.

"Oh, *Bomberman*! Awesome! I'm in!" Her eyes lit up as she raised her hand to volunteer.

"Wish you could've been here a little sooner. Now

I have to plug everything in all over again," Grandma complained. But she couldn't hide the amusement in her voice.

As I watched her, and Gon just behind her, my heart began to race like it was marching for a revolution. I tapped my fingers on my knees in time to its beat. No matter how deeply I delved inside myself, right now, all I found was warmth and joy...and I wished I could bask in it forever.

And so, two days later, our yearly summer trip came to an end. Whenever we left my grandparents' house, family tradition dictated that we use the front door and go the long way around.

"See you next year, Grandma and Grandpa."

"Or next month, if you don't want to wait that long," Grandma replied.

"She's right, you know," Grandpa nodded.

"We can make it a monthly thing if you pay me," my mother snarked, but we all laughed and ignored her.

Setting that aside...Grandma had brought my dear friend outside to see me off, and it was time to say farewell.

"Gon."

He looked up at me, and I gave him a big hug, nuzzling my face in his fur. He was still just as warm as I remembered.

"Gon..."

My voice trembled quietly, but the words on my tongue ebbed like the tide. I just couldn't say goodbye. Then I felt a hand on my head, and I knew it was Grandma's without even looking.

"I'll send you lots of pictures, sweetheart." Her voice was painfully gentle. "Okay?"

"...Okay."

I could tell she was trying to make me feel better, and I couldn't bear to look her in the eye. Then, at last, I straightened up...and my mother clapped me on the shoulder.

"No tantrum? My little girl's all grown up!"

"Shut up, *Mother*," I shot back.

Then my sister looked up at me, her eyes wide. I looked back at her. "What's wrong?"

"Nothing..."

She seemed to want to say something, but oddly enough, she held back. Curious though I was, I didn't press her on it. Instead, I faced forward and started walking. I knew if I looked over my shoulder, I'd run back and give Gon another hug.

So I walked around from the front of the house to the driveway in the back...where Grandma and Grandpa were already waiting for us. Again.

"This tradition is so utterly pointless..."

With one last energetic wave, we piled into my father's newly polished car. Then we buckled our seatbelts and drove off. And as the vibrations massaged my back, I felt a strange sense of accomplishment.

I thought long and hard about Gon, but in the end, I never managed to get the words out. Still, that in itself was a valid choice. Not everything had to be so cut and dried. Just because I couldn't express the indescribable feelings in my heart, it didn't mean they weren't still there. I wasn't heartless—I was a human being with emotions of my own.

And after we arrived back at home, those emotions spurred me to action. I got out of the car, turned to face the road, and screamed with every fiber of my being until my lungs gave out.

"AAAAAAAAAAAAAAAAAAAAAAHHHHH!"

I screamed and screamed until my brain begged for oxygen, until my throat was sore, until my ears started to ring. Sweat came pouring out of me like I was back in that sauna. But for once, I felt *alive*. A new sun was forming behind my eyes, lighting up all the dusty corners of my mind.

Ignoring the alarmed stares I was surely getting from the rest of my family, I then immediately placed a call on my cell phone. She answered so fast, she reminded me of the way Gon would always race to the door to greet me. The thought made me chuckle.

In a voice as dry as a rocky riverbed, I said to her: "Adachi...I'm home."

"**H**EY, GRANDPA, does this place have any famous souvenirs?" I ask my grandpa out in the yard.

"Well, our dried persimmons are fairly well known," he answers promptly.

"Dried persimmons...?"

Sounds like a pretty boring souvenir to me. But Yachi loves anything sweet, so maybe she'd actually like them a lot.

"Oh, wait," he continues as he adds more water to the water garden terrarium where the pet fish live. "Now that I think of it, they're out of season right now."

"Oh." I guess if anyone tried to dry them during the summer, they'd just rot. In this heat, even *people* turn to mush.

"So, looking for souvenirs, are you?"

"I wanted to buy something for a friend."

"I see, I see."

He clears away the flowers on the water's surface, then walks back and heads for the kitchen. Confused, I follow behind him.

When we get there, we find Grandma chopping up onions at the speed of light. "How can I help you two?"

"Just a moment and I'll be out of your hair."

Grandpa opens the freezer, and a gust of chilly air washes over us. Feels nice.

"I think we still had some..."

Then he starts taking everything out of the freezer and setting it on the floor. This earns him some side-eye from Grandma. "Just put it all back when you're done, please."

"I will, I will," Grandpa answers absently as he lines up all the frozen fish. Then he sees something in the back and his eyes light up. "I knew it! Good job, me. I'm so smart."

He pats himself on the back like he's five years old. Then he pulls out a Ziploc baggie, opens it, and takes out one of the little lumps bundled up in paper and cling wrap.

"Still had some homemade dried persimmons in the freezer, if that'll do. You're welcome to take 'em."

"Ooooh!" I didn't realize what they were until he told me. Boy, are they cold.

"Hah hah hah!" Grandpa looks pretty pleased with himself. Meanwhile, Grandma rolls her eyes.

And that's the story of how I got a souvenir for Yachi.

Back at home, I'm ready to give Yachi her present, but then it hits me: I don't know where she lives! Normally, she always comes over to my house and never the other way around, so I don't have her phone number either... I pace up and down the hallway and try to think of what to do.

Maybe she'll show up if I wait long enough, I think to myself. So I sit around and wait, fidgeting. Sometimes I go to the kitchen and check to make sure the dried persimmons are still in the freezer. Then I go back to my room and wait some more.

The next morning, Yachi still isn't here. Usually, I get to see her at least three times a day! I start pacing down the hall again, but then my big sister wakes up and sees me. She's got a bad case of bedhead, and her hair's sticking out in all directions like a lion.

"Settle down out here."

Hmph. How about *you* go settle your hair? "Well, Yachi's still not here."

"Have you tried calling for her?" she suggests, like it's obvious.

"But *how*?"

"Let's see..."

Yawning, she walks into the kitchen. What the...? I start to wonder if maybe she's still half-asleep. But then she comes back carrying a bag of honey candies.

"Just run around holding this bag over your head."

"...What does that have to do with Yachi?"

"Trust me, it works."

She pushes the bag into my hands and stumbles off. Then she staggers sideways and hits her head on the wall. She's really not a morning person, is she? How pathetic.

But forget about her—is this really going to lure Yachi to our house? How does she know for sure that it works? Skeptical, I twirl the bag in my hands, and the cartoon bee on the package happily spins around.

"Hmmmm..."

Reluctantly, I hold the bag of candy over my head. Nobody's watching, but it still feels super dumb. Then I run down the hallway. With both hands occupied, I feel vulnerable and insecure. My face burns and itches like I'm outside in the sun.

Part of me is convinced this is pointless, but...I can't shake the thought that Yachi might really show up. For her, nothing in this world is impossible.

...Wait, what the?

On my third lap, I realize there's a second set of footsteps right behind me. I look over my shoulder, and sure enough, there she is. We freeze, our hands raised over our heads in the same pose. Our eyes meet.

"Little!"

Then she runs right over to me, her arms outstretched, and...she doesn't seem to be slowing down at all. Should I be worried?

Turns out, the answer is yes. She tackles me at full speed.

"Gwegh!"

Together, we fall to the hallway floor. Her hair flows down onto me, and as it sweeps over my skin, it absorbs all my extra heat.

"Oh, Little, I missed you!"

"Whoa, whoa!"

She hugs me and rubs her cheek against mine, squishing our faces together. I start to feel dizzy, and my face feels hot. She smells like something I've never smelled before—I don't know how to describe it, but it feels like a crisp breeze, or like something metallic wafting under my nose. I breathe it in, and now it feels like it's behind my eyeballs.

Just then, she stops nuzzling me and looks at me, confused. "Aren't you going to do it back?"

"Wha? You want me to?"

"Squishy, squishy!"

She rubs her chin against mine. Who taught you to do this stuff, anyway?

"Squishy...squishy..." Awkwardly, I nuzzle her back, which feels even more embarrassing than being on the receiving end. Not sure why. My cheeks burn like I've been splashed with hot water.

Meanwhile, Yachi keeps on squishing. She must be really happy to see me... When I stop to think about it, I get all self-conscious and my mind goes blank.

And so we spend a while right there on the hallway floor.

"I didn't realize you were back, Little," Yachi says after we get up. She smiles like she's not even embarrassed—seriously, how is that possible? Then I realize she's already holding the bag of candy.

"Um...yeah." I'm tempted to ask why the candy lured her out, or how she sensed it at all, but I decide not to think too hard about it. "I brought you a souvenir and everything."

"Is it something delicious?"

Grrrr! You don't care about me at all, do you? You just want your dumb gift! I should have known. "Yeah, I think so. This way."

I lead her into the kitchen, where I find my big sister

slumped over the table. Now her hair's fanned out in all directions like a jellyfish.

"Oh! Shimamura-san!"

Yachi runs over and tackles her, slamming her forehead into my sister's legs. Then she floats down to the floor. I swear, it's almost like gravity doesn't affect her.

"Nnnh?" My sister looks up from the table, her eyes and mouth both half-open. "Sleepy..."

"That's what you get for staying up so late. Lord knows you weren't spending that time hitting the books," Mom scoffs as she cleans the sink.

"I was on the phone with a friend...and every time I tried to hang up, she'd start talking about something else," my sister whines as she slumps back over the table.

Whatever—forget about her! I open the freezer, grab the Ziploc baggie, and pull out a persimmon. It's so cold, it feels like it might freeze my fingers. Perfect for summer. I pull off the cling wrap and paper so I can show Yachi what it looks like.

"It's very wrinkly," she says, stating the obvious.

"It's a dried persimmon."

"Persimmon?" She tilts her head.

I had a feeling she wouldn't know about them, so I eagerly start to explain. "Right now it's frozen, but once it thaws—"

"Chomp!"

"Aah!"

Before I can finish, she sinks her teeth into the persimmon and starts gnawing aggressively at the frozen fruit. Eegh! Before I can react, she starts to smile. "Sweet and delicious indeed!"

She looks like the happiest girl in the whole world... She really does love her sweets.

"Hmmm..."

You know, she may look like a fairy-tale character, but if she was in *Hansel and Gretel*, she'd probably devour the witch's whole house.

"So you like it?"

"It's very good."

"My grandpa made these all by himself," I brag, as if it's *my* accomplishment somehow.

"Oh, I see," she nods as she gnaws. She smiles like she's savoring the sweetness, and then her pretty eyes wander to me. "Why don't you have some, Little?"

"Wha?!"

She offers me the other side of the dried persimmon. I guess she wants us to eat it together, but...it's frozen! I can't tear off a piece, so I'll have to gnaw it like she's doing! Seriously?! I don't know if I should... That's not how you're supposed to eat it...

Perplexed, I look around the room, but my mom's busy cleaning, and my sister's still a jellyfish. Yachi and I are in our own little world together.

The morning sun streams in through the window, melting my brain. Like a moth drawn to the flame, I lean in and gently bite down on the other side of the persimmon. Her eyes and mouth are inches away, and our noses are practically touching. Meanwhile, she gnaws away without a care in the world, her hair and forehead brushing against mine.

My throat tightens as I tense up. What'll happen when we meet in the middle...?

My lips burn so hot, I can practically feel them defrosting the persimmon.

After the phone call, I hastily brushed my hair. I still hadn't put on any makeup or even changed my clothes. *Gah, hurry up!* My body felt like molasses, and it was driving me insane. But when the urgency fell in sync with my racing heartbeat, it gave me a pleasant little thrill... and I almost felt like dancing.

Time to go see Shimamura.

4. The Complications of Love

"**Y**OU KNOW, I've been thinking about this for a while, but...if I'm catlike, then you're definitely doglike."

"...What?" *I am?*

No "hi," no "how are you"—*this* was the first thing Shimamura said to me after I raced over to her house. Was it because I was sweating and panting? Pretty sure this wasn't the first time she made this comment either.

"Hmmm..."

She folded her arms in contemplation and looked at me. I stood there in the entryway to her house, shoes still on, and blinked back at her.

I hadn't seen her in two or three days, so looking at her was like looking at the moon—my only observation was *Wow, pretty*. She seemed so vibrant and full of life...

or was it just because I hadn't seen her in a while? Her weird taste in T-shirts, however, hadn't changed a bit. Today, she was wearing one with a big cartoon sandwich on the front.

"On second thought, I'd better not."

She closed her eyes in disappointment. I wasn't sure what sort of internal argument she was having with herself, but I couldn't just let it slide. "Wh-what is it?"

"I just don't think it's, you know, very nice," she replied, nodding to herself. But this didn't answer my question, and I was starting to think she was dodging it on purpose.

"Okay, well, now I *really* wanna know."

"I don't know... I probably shouldn't do it..."

Was she serious or just trying to play coy? "It... It's fine. Just do it," I pressed. I wasn't sure if it had anything to do with me, but I was curious either way. The more I learned about Shimamura, the happier I was overall.

"You sure?"

"Bring it...on...?"

I was trying to imitate the thing Shimamura said a while back, though I couldn't possibly spread my arms out like she did. I could feel sweat dripping all over my body, and my shoulders were trembling.

"Okay, then. Here."

She offered me her hand, palm side up. But she wasn't

holding anything. I thought maybe there was another step involved, so I waited anxiously...but she didn't move. She just stared at me like she was waiting for *me* to do something.

Is this what I think it is...?

Timidly, I placed my hand on her palm. I was her dog, and she wanted me to shake... My face burned hotter and hotter as it all clicked.

"Perfect," Shimamura nodded, satisfied. "Anyway, you must be even sweatier than I am. Come on in and let's cool off."

With this ritual (?) now complete, she pulled her hand away, then turned and led me into the house. Classic Shimamura. As usual, she had her own set of priorities. Frankly, I was almost impressed. *Ugh, I'm such a terminal case.*

As I pulled off my shoes with my now-empty hands, I called after her.

"Shimamura!" Her name left my lips, traveled to her ears, and made her turn back. Why did this invisible connection always make me smile? "Welcome home."

I wanted to save it for when we were in person.

Her gaze wandered for a moment, and then a tiny smile crept up on her lips.

"I was gonna say you're being dramatic, but then I

remembered *I'm* the one who said 'I'm home' in the first place." She spun on her heel, turning her whole body in my direction as gracefully as a dancer. "I came back for you, Adachi."

Like a lump of burning charcoal, a piece of my hardened heart popped, and a sharp pain shot through me.

"Whoa!"

I could feel the blood frothing in my wrists. My eyes throbbed in time with my pulse, quavering.

Shimamura...had pulled me into a hug.

AFDSAKGSK;H!!! I had initiated hugs with her multiple times before, but now for the first time ever, *she* was hugging *me,* and I was FREAKING OUT!!! *ASJDHGJLFK!!!*

It felt like I was drowning. I was so limp, I wasn't even sure I still had bones in my shoulders. Meanwhile, she rubbed my back and gently ran her fingers through my hair. If she was trying to disable me completely, it was working. I was scared my frothing blood might start leaking from my mouth if I wasn't careful.

Then she clapped me on the back three times, and I started coughing.

"Just kidding," she grinned as she casually stepped away.

"Wha...?" The disappointment was so immense, I couldn't quite hold it in.

"Oh... Ha ha... Good one," I choked out hastily as I fought to get my emotions under control—a daunting task since my vision was spinning. Clutching my frothing wrist, I found myself compelled to ask: "Shimamura, are you in a good mood today?"

"Hm? No, not at all," she replied airily. "If anything, I faced reality and had my heart broken." For a moment, her gaze lowered with her voice. "But..."

She seemed to swallow the rest of her sentence. And as the words slid back down her throat, the look on her face was sorrowful, yet beautiful. Suppressing the urge to wrap my arms around her, I followed her down the hallway to her room on the first floor.

When we arrived, her little sister took one look at me and her expression darkened. Then she swiftly slipped past me and out of the room. It was clear I wasn't welcome here.

Frankly, I still wasn't comfortable around Little Shimamura. We were too similar, which meant we were both probably thinking the same thing. And considering how I felt about her, it was no surprise she wasn't excited to see me either. She probably wanted me gone.

"I don't know what to do about her," Shimamura murmured, smiling stiffly.

Part of me felt guilty, but at the same time, I refused to let anyone else hog her, not even her own family.

"Don't mind the clutter, by the way. We only just got back, so we haven't had time to put any stuff away."

"It's cool."

Not like a single suitcase worth of clothes was much of a mess, anyway. She switched on the electric fan and turned it toward me; I inclined my head in gratitude.

"You know, when I called, I wasn't expecting you to come over literally right this minute," she laughed as she sat with her legs splayed out.

Admittedly, yes, I did rush over kind of fast, but that was hardly out of the ordinary for me. After all that time, I couldn't possibly wait a single second longer. Like a paper football, her words gave me a hard flick and sent me flying.

"Hmmm..."

Stroking her chin, she shot me a sidelong glance, then held out her palm again. Slowly, timidly, I put my hand in hers.

"Good!" Again, she seemed satisfied. And for some reason, my heart fluttered.

This time, I curled my fingers and held tight. We were both a little sweaty in this heat, but that was proof that she was right there. Even *I* could see it, and I wasn't looking directly at her. Likewise, she made no move to pull away—she just sat there at my side. Meanwhile, the fan was blowing over our shoulders.

"So, um, how'd it go?"

"How'd what go?"

I wasn't sure what to say, since I didn't really know what it was like. "How was, um, your grandpa's house?"

"Oh, you know..." She averted her eyes. Apparently, she didn't want to talk about it. "It was fine, I guess. So anyway, did you wear that swimsuit?"

I could tell she had purposely changed the subject, and it made me a tiny bit sad to know she wasn't comfortable opening up to me. What more did I need to do to reach that stage with her? Furthermore, what did she mean by that question? Was she asking if I'd already worn it out somewhere?

Do I count the time I took photos in my room...? That probably counts, right? Thinking about it made my brain turn to mush, and I could barely get my tongue to cooperate.

"I've...only worn it twice."

Once for the photo shoot, and...

"Well, that's no good! You gotta wear it more than that!" she replied teasingly.

If you want me to wear it more, then give me more excuses to wear it. I grasped the hem of my shirt, then thought better of it. *Too soon.*

Just then, Shimamura's phone rang. She started to reach for it, then felt resistance and looked back at me.

Our joined hands formed a bridge between us. For a brief moment, she opened her mouth to speak, but ultimately, she chose to pull me with her to grab her phone. I waited silently, toppling over in an effort to keep hold of her.

The phone only jingled once, so it was probably just an email, but...from who? Was it...that girl from the festival? Who was she, and what sort of relationship did she have with Shimamura? She still hadn't explained it to me, and every time I remembered this unsolved mystery, it made me want to play detective. But a white-knuckled interrogation would only end in an icy stare, and the thought made my blood run cold. I didn't need to hold myself back when my own imagination crushed any lingering trace of courage I otherwise might have had.

She looked at her phone screen and chuckled. *What's so funny?* I hated the thought that someone else was making her smile. My gut smoldered darkly, filling my chest with smoke. I could *feel* it polluting me.

As the smoke billowed inside me, Shimamura noticed my expression and showed me her phone. I wasn't sure I should look, but I looked nonetheless. There on the screen was a photo of a dog and an old woman making a funny face.

"This is my grandma, and this is her pet dog," she

explained gently. It felt like she was introducing me to her family.

The dog looked really, really old, and its left eye was all milky—probably blind, if I had to guess. The old woman (Shimamura's grandmother, apparently) was leaning close to the dog's face, imitating its expression by pouting her lips. I...wasn't really sure what to say, honestly. "She, uh, looks like a real goofball."

"She's my mom's mom, so, yeah," Shimamura sighed wryly.

At this, I thought back to what I knew of Mrs. Shimamura: a rather playful woman in her own right. In that case, was Shimamura secretly just as goofy as her mother and grandmother...? *No, not exactly,* I thought to myself as I gazed at her warm expression from the side. I could feel my tongue quivering in the back of my mouth.

She's so cute!

Was it because I'd yearned for her so desperately over the past three days, or had something about her changed? I wasn't sure. But now all the little things I used to take for granted were affecting me especially hard. There was a warm, peaceful ocean in my chest, and my whole body felt like it was floating—a little scary, yes, but I wanted to relish the moment as long as I could. This warmth was far more gentle than any summer sun.

"So, what now? Feels like I have to ask this question every time you come over."

"Huh? What do you mean?"

"Well, what do you want to do together?" she asked, looking around the room. Her gaze drifted from the TV to the bookshelf to the video games. "Aren't you bored?"

"No," I replied, leaning against her shoulder. When our bodies were this close, frankly, I didn't have the mental capacity to feel bored. Our faces were only inches apart, and her eyes looked so big and round... They seemed to pierce straight through me.

"Well, okay, then."

She relaxed her shoulders, and my head settled on top. A strand of her hair was tickling my face, driving home just how *close* she was. And as I grew more flustered, our arms brushed together, rustling my clothes...

Then I remembered: *Oh, that's right.*

"Nnnn..."

Now I had a choice to make: stay comfy, or venture outside that comfort zone? Sure, I could happily remain right where I was, but maybe Shimamura was already bored. I didn't want to selfishly focus on my own happiness—I wanted to be considerate of hers too. That was an important part of *opening my eyes to the people around me*, which was what Shimamura said she wanted me to do.

But no matter how "open" my eyes were, I was pretty sure I would only ever use them to find her.

Truth be told, it was a dangerous move. If I messed up, it could make things weird. But even the most risky of gambles could, in theory, pay off. That was simply how the game was meant to be played.

With this subconscious encouragement, I rose to my feet and grabbed the hem of my shirt. As a scarlet spiral swirled around in my skull, I pulled my shirt off. Then I saw Shimamura's wide-eyed stare fixed on me, and my panic began to spin like a wheel. The resulting steam empowered me to whip the rest of my clothes off all at once. No time to fiddle with zippers.

I let my outerwear fall to the floor, then nervously stumbled over and stood in front of her. I could hear my blood pumping in my ears as the temperature in my body skyrocketed.

I was standing there in nothing but the swimsuit I'd worn under my clothes.

"Wh-what do you think…?"

To the surprise of no one, I wasn't bold enough to strike a pose. Rubbing my feet together, I tried to gauge her reaction, but couldn't bear to look up. Then, as I stared at the floor, I heard her ask: "You were wearing your swimsuit the whole time?"

I nodded.

"Specifically so you could show it off?"

I nodded, more faintly this time, but that wasn't entirely why. I didn't want to *show it off*, per se—I just wanted her to see it. "So, um... Thoughts...?"

At last, I managed to look up a little...and found Shimamura staring at my chest. "Interesting."

Interesting?! What kind of interesting, *exactly?!*

"The colors are a lot brighter in person, huh?"

She leaned in close and scrutinized my bikini bottom. *AKDGHLDSHLHDG!!!* My vision was swaying so hard, I could only assume my eyeballs were literally spinning in their sockets.

"Uhh, uhhhh, y-yeah, uhh... Blue and white, ha ha..."

"And your skin is super pale too."

She patted my thigh and my leg nearly flinched. The blood was rising to my head, making me dizzy. I staggered backward.

"Oh, gosh, are you okay?"

"Aaauuhhhaauhhh..."

"I take it that's a no, huh?" She nodded pensively.

Wh-whose fault do you think that is, missy?! "Th-that was... That was sexual harassment...wasn't it?"

I meant it like a joke, but it came out sounding like a serious question.

"*What*?" She laughed. "No it wasn't! I just touched your thigh!"

"Yeah, and that's...s-sexual harassment..."

Slowly, I sank to my knees and put my hands in my lap like I was attending a formal tea ceremony. I could feel my stiff shoulders and back twitching aggressively. The skin around my collarbone was so tight, it felt like my skeleton was trying to make a run for it.

"Ha ha ha ha!" Just then, Shimamura burst out laughing. Startled, I looked up at her, and she smiled. "You're so funny."

"Oh...yeah...ha ha..."

Well, at least she's not bored, I...guess...?

"Anyway, um...that reminds me..." *Agh, what am I saying?!* "Wanna take a bath?"

"A bath?"

"Yeah."

"At my house?"

"Yeah. Both of us."

"*What*?"

"Like, at the same time..."

It felt like my eyes were on fire. Light popped in my vision—twice.

"So...you wanna take a bath together?" she asked, mulling it over. Her hesitation didn't surprise me, but this time I wasn't going to back down.

"Well, I mean...I'm already wearing it..."

"Wearing what?"

"My swimsuit..."

It made sense, right? Bath, water, swimsuit. Okay, maybe it was a major stretch, but I didn't have anything else to work with. My only option was to act casual and pray that Shimamura would come around with her usual "Eh, okay."

After a few moments...she burst out laughing. Again. Clutching her stomach.

"What are you *talking* about? You're such a weirdo!"

"I...I am?" My voice cracked like it was trying to make me sound stupid on purpose.

"You *are*! The way you think, the way you act—it's *totally* weird. Like, how the heck do you come up with this stuff? Because it's just so uniquely *you*."

As far as she was concerned, I was weird inside and out. I would have liked to at least be normal on the outside, but this was perhaps asking too much, considering I was currently wearing a swimsuit in someone else's bedroom. And since I was kneeling, I could feel the bottoms of my feet pressed up against my butt.

God, I'm so uncomfortable. Should I put my shirt back on? For some reason, the thought of redressing myself in front of Shimamura made me want to die. Why was this somehow different from when I was stripping? I clutched my bare biceps and writhed.

"Okay, then," she said in a cheerful tone. "Seeing as you came prepared, let's go take ourselves a bath!"

"Wha?!"

That wasn't the "Eh, okay" I'd hoped for. No, it was *even better*. Part of me was overjoyed that she appreciated my careful planning, but another part of me was alarmed that she would notice it at all. Clearly, she was plenty weird herself... Then my outlook swung back to positive: *That's just Shimamura for you.*

"I'm not sure I see the point of it, but...oh, well."

As she spoke, she rose to her feet. Likewise, I shot up like a bullet. She smirked at me, then turned and led me out of the room.

Partway there, the nerves made my stomach cramp, and my ears started to ring so loud, it actually drowned out the wail of the cicadas. I was so stiff, I was barely breathing; if I were to fall into the deep end of a swimming pool, I'd hit the bottom and probably never rise again. This was an emotion I'd felt a lot in the time since I first met Shimamura... Honestly, it was a miracle I'd survived this long.

As we passed by the living room, I caught a glimpse of Shimamura's mother unpacking her luggage. Then

Shimamura called out to her: "I'm gonna go take a bath."

"A bath? In the middle of the day? Don't you have anything better to do?" Mrs. Shimamura scoffed over her shoulder. Then she saw me standing next to her daughter. "Oh, Adachi-chan, I didn't know you were here."

"Sorry to intrude," I replied, bowing my head.

"You're so polite! I wish my daughter would...learn from...your..." Her words petered out. "Whyza swimsuit?"

It was, of course, a perfectly reasonable question to pose to a teenage girl standing in your hallway in a bikini. "Whyza swimsuit," indeed. *Ugh, I totally should've put my clothes back on.*

"She came over to take a bath with me," Shimamura answered in my place.

"For the record, I just thought it would be fun... Mostly I wanted to show off my new bikini..." I mumbled in my own defense.

But Mrs. Shimamura didn't seem to hear either of us. "Hmmm," she murmured. Her reaction seemed unfavorable...or perhaps just confused. No surprise there. "Looks like my daughter's oddball personality is contagious. Dear me, what's a mother to do?" she lamented dramatically, as she was often wont to do.

I looked over at Shimamura to find her staring at her

mother with a sneer that said "Hypocrite much?" But this gave me pause. Never before had I seen Shimamura give someone such a dirty look. Was she always this emotional? *Wait, that's not how I should put it.* Was she always so...open with her emotions?

Perhaps something meaningful had happened while she was at her grandparents' house. If so, then judging from her behavior earlier, she most likely wasn't going to talk to me about it. If only I could have been there in person to see it for myself... Maybe then I wouldn't feel so left out.

I never should have let her leave me for so long.

Out of the corner of my eye, I watched Adachi slowly transform into a crab. She sat cross-legged, her mouth submerged under the water, bubbles periodically rising to the surface. Her gaze darted restlessly between me and her knees, and her face was already flushed red. So, yeah, I was mildly concerned that she might not be doing okay.

"Can't remember the last time I took a bath during the daytime," I mused to myself.

She nodded quietly, making small ripples in the water's surface.

"And I've certainly never taken one with a friend from school before." That is, unless you counted that time Tarumi and I took a bath together when we were really little.

Adachi nodded again, but I could tell she was happier this time—proof that I had gained a deeper understanding of her.

And so there we were, in the bathtub at my house. At least it was bigger than the one at Grandpa's.

Naturally, it would be...unfair?...if I was the only one naked, so I went and put on my school swimsuit. Truth be told, it felt extremely strange to wear this at my own house. And this tub *really* wasn't big enough for both of us to sit side by side. Maybe if I was with my sister, but two teenagers? It was a tight fit, to put it mildly. We both kept bumping our elbows and knees, especially Adachi.

"You sure don't look comfortable," I commented. *Sorta defeats the purpose of a nice relaxing bath, doesn't it?* At my comment, she shamefully buried her face even lower. More bubbles rose to the surface. *Still in crab mode, I see.*

"You know, I kinda miss the days when you used to be chill."

What happened to the girl I first met in the gym loft? It felt like I'd barely gotten a glimpse of her before she turned all antsy. It made me wonder if she had some kind of cursed armor equipped, like in an RPG.

From what I'd heard from other people, Adachi used to be really aloof back in junior high. Then, after she met me, she... *Wait, what?* That would mean it was *my* fault that she went psy—er, stopped being grumpy. *Hmmm.*

"So, belated question: What made you want to take a bath, anyways?" The thought had only just occurred to me. Maybe the steam was melting my brain.

Water dripped from the ends of her hair as she modestly concealed her new bikini behind her knees. "I thought a bath would...bring us closer together," she answered, a few words at a time, like a slow stream of bubbles.

"Whyzat?" I asked, imitating my mother.

She blew bubbles in the water like she didn't have an answer. To be fair, I sure wouldn't take a bath with someone I wasn't close to, but...to me, the order felt a little bit backward. That said, friendships founded on strict rules were pretty much guaranteed to fall apart sooner or later, so...

"Well..."

"Yes?"

She faltered, blushing. Then she sank into the water, blowing bubbles furiously, her eyes darting every which way. I shot her an inquiring look; she held my gaze for a long moment, then finally conceded and lifted her head above the water.

"Being naked makes you...vulnerable...and it's important to be vulnerable with your friends," she mumbled as her hair slapped at the water's surface.

"Riiiight! I get it now. Wait, but we're not naked!" I laughed. Then she sank below the water again. "Uh oh."

This time she lowered herself all the way to her forehead. Then came the bubbles—a *lot* of bubbles. If she sank a tiny bit lower, her hair would float on the surface like a jellyfish... Why did the thought excite me? This was no time to fantasize about a human-sized jellyfish! If I left Adachi to her own devices, she'd probably drown!

Instead, I decided to haul her up like a salvage ship. Problem being, I didn't know what part of her I should grab onto. Her hips? She'd probably accuse me of "sexual harassment" again. Her armpits? No, that'd be even worse! What about her neck? ...Now it was starting to feel less like a rescue maneuver and more like a pro wrestling technique.

"Hmmmm...mmm...mmm..."

My gaze trailed over her bare back. Her skin was so pale and untanned... Just then, I thought of something I'd always wanted to try. I reached out, grabbed the strings of her bikini top, and tugged.

This got an immediate response. Adachi shot up out of the water, splashing waves in every direction as she stared at me, wide-eyed. The attack was super-effective! If only it was this easy to get the fish to bite.

"Wha…buh…buh…?!" She spluttered at me, her back against the edge of the tub, one hand pressed to the wall. Plus, she flailed her legs so much, you'd think she was drowning. She was getting water all over the walls.

Uh oh. Did I go too far? "I'm sorry, I'm sorry!" I apologized, just in case.

At this, she relaxed slightly and sat back down. "It's fine," she mumbled, staring down solemnly at the water.

Silence fell as the two of us sat there, submerged up to our shoulders in hot water. To be perfectly honest, I was ready to get out. Why were we acting like a couple of children in here? At our age, I'd expected we'd behave a bit more…ladylike, I guess. But my friendship with Adachi was an eternal roller coaster.

The sound of dripping water seemed so distant, almost like it was raining outside. When I looked up, I realized the ceiling was hazy with steam. It almost felt like we were at a hot spring somewhere; I could practically hear the *clonk* of the traditional wooden buckets. Water dripped from my hair and streaked sideways down my forehead and nose.

"…Adachi, are you trying to be kind to me?"

I decided to ask on a whim since we were in private.

Normally, I'd be way too ashamed to ask this directly, so I probably would have couched it in softer words. But I wanted to know what it was that made people choose kindness. Where did it come from? Certainly not from obligation, I knew that much. But if I could trace it to its source, then maybe I could learn how to do it myself...or so I hoped, anyway.

At this—"Bffgghh!"—Adachi splashed me with water. "What, you don't think I'm nice?"

She gazed at me sadly, like an egg on the verge of cracking. Her eyes were so puffy, she looked like she was about to cry; naturally, this was all the answer I needed. Still, there was something truly refreshing about the way Adachi wore her heart on her sleeve.

"I don't knoooow," I replied in a singsong voice, teasing her. With a smirk, I turned my back to her.

I could feel her panicking just behind me. I didn't want to stress her out *too* much, so I turned back to let her know that she *was,* in fact, a nice girl. But just then, my forehead collided with something—with *her* forehead, apparently? I had no time to feel the pain, however, because she wrapped her arms around me. And because we were both in our swimsuits, this resulted in a very tight hug.

I could feel her perfect skin directly against mine. As the hot water splashed and danced and shifted all around us, the only constant was Adachi. Then the water fell still...and the heat began to build.

Admittedly, I had to wonder: *Why is this always your default reaction?* But to her credit, maybe this was the only way she knew how to express herself. Maybe she was trying to be as nice as she possibly could... If so, then it wasn't much different from usual. Did that mean she was just really nice all the time? *Dang, that's impressive.*

Unfortunately, this hug was starting to hurt.

"Uh, Adachi?" *Your chin's really digging into my shoulder, and I'm scared it's gonna bury itself there.* "Helloooo? Adachiiii?"

I patted her lightly on the shoulder, willing her to ease up a little, but she didn't respond. She was frozen like a statue. So I had no choice but to push her shoulders and peel her off of me. I was worried maybe she passed out or something, but thankfully, I could see her eyes moving. She was still breathing too...but she was trembling. Her eyes and lips twitched, and then...

"Gaaagh!"

"Aaaaah!"

She began to babble incoherently as she reaffixed herself to me—more tightly this time, as if to prevent my escape. She even wrapped her *legs* around me. Meanwhile, her head lolled from side to side.

"Whoa, whoa, whoa!"

She had seemingly turned into a zombie, and as I held her, I began to panic. Was she going to bite my jugular? Would I become one of the infected? I didn't want that. If I turned into another Adachi, who would help us calm down in a crisis? Still, even if she *did* sometimes create problems, at least she knew how to take action at all. Clearly, our friendship needed at least one Adachi.

As I ruminated on this, I sensed her lips moving near my ear. Curious, I listened carefully. And then, in a tiny voice, she whispered...

"I wuv you..."

Punctuated by the *plip, plip* of water dripping into the tub.

"I...love you...love...love you...so much..."

"...Huh?" Water trickled down between our bodies as my arms went limp and sank beneath the surface. My head was spinning. I couldn't process the words.

"Nnngh...ggmmh...mmgghh..."

"......Wait, what?"

She was groaning an awful lot, so I pushed her off me again. But this time, the problem was plain to see.

"*Oh, god, she passed out!*"

This was exactly the scenario I was afraid of. I could practically see the steam rising from her head... Hastily,

I pulled her out of the tub and dragged her out of the bathroom to the hallway, where I laid her down. Then, without pausing to towel myself off, I dashed straight to the kitchen, to my mother.

"Mom! Help! Adachi passed out in the bathtub!"

"Oh, for crying out loud, you dumb kids!"

Despite her insults, she swiftly grabbed a washcloth and soaked it in cold water. Then she grabbed a sports drink from the fridge and ran back with me to the hallway, which was now slick with my own watery footprints. Working quickly, my mother wiped down Adachi's body with the cold washcloth, paying special attention to her neck and feet. Only then did Adachi regain consciousness.

"Shimamura," she murmured, looking at me. *That's my Adachi, all right.*

Once she confirmed Adachi had recovered, my mother rounded on me. "Hey birdbrain, try not to kill her, would you?" And with that, she walked off.

Excuse me? I didn't force her to stay in the tub that long! Annoyed, I kept a close eye on Adachi. And as I watched her, I could feel a question rising with the steam:

What did she say to me just now?

Only Adachi knew the answer, and right now, she was in no condition to tell me.

"You sure you don't want to stay and cool off a little longer?" Shimamura asked kindly as she walked me outside.

"Nah, I'm all good now," I replied, shaking my head. I decided it was smarter for me to leave early rather than run the risk of embarrassing myself even more.

To tell the truth, I didn't realize "passing out" was something that actually happened in real life. I didn't remember much of what happened after my mind went fuzzy... *She told me she nursed me back to health, but...god, I didn't completely humiliate myself or something, did I?!* I was too terrified to ask. Maybe I just wasn't ready for non-solo bathing activities.

My head still felt heavy, and my fingertips were numb. My mind was sluggish, still smothered in a thick layer of steam. In this condition, there was no telling what sorts of things I might have said to Shimamura... But since I was capable of recognizing that much, it was probably safe for me to go home.

I set my hands on the handlebars of my bike and looked over my shoulder. With wet hair and a towel around her neck, Shimamura looked strikingly different from usual, and I was too shy to look at her. No makeup, no hair products, and a shirt that clung tightly to her curves... Flustered, I stared at the ground. There were stars in my eyes, and not just because I hit my head. I shook them away, then hopped onto my bike. Yes, I was going home for the day, but...

"Can I...call you tonight?" I asked, a tiny bit more confident than usual.

"Of course," Shimamura replied, with a toothy grin that caught me off guard.

Instantly, I was captivated. It was an innocent, pure smile—one that came naturally rather than consciously, one that revealed her true nature, and one that set my heart alight.

"Bye-bye," she said, like a much younger version of herself, as she waved at me.

"Bye."

"And remember, you have to keep your eyes on the road when you're riding your bike. So this is where we part ways, okay?"

Somehow she was one step ahead of me. Fireworks lit up in my already flushed cheeks, popping and crackling. Meanwhile, I started pedaling my bike. As requested, I wasn't going to look back this time. Nope, not this time.

But I really, really, *really* wanted to.

Suppressing the impulse, I thought instead of—you

guessed it—Shimamura. I reflected on all of the day's moments, pedaling mindlessly as I sank deeper and deeper into the memories.

As it turned out, I was still a distracted driver, even when I was facing forward.

I stood alone in the dry summer breeze. The wind seemed to clear the steam from my mind. Then, suddenly, I realized:

Oh, I get it now. Adachi loves me.

Assuming she wasn't just joking around back there, of course. But considering the state she was in at the time, she probably didn't have the mental capacity to tell any jokes.

"Hmm..."

Maybe *that* was the reason she treated me so kindly. As the realization set in, it sent a shudder across my skin. Before I knew it, I was clutching my elbow, cradling myself. My vision seemed to zoom out, spreading to every corner of town.

"*Now* I get it..."

It was the simplest answer and the most logical motivation. Looking back, she was *so obvious* about it too.

Why else would she be so obsessed with me? Why else would she have a breakdown when she found out I spent time with someone else? Yes, it all made perfect sense... and yet...

"Hmmmm."

Strands of wet hair slapped against my cheek, tickling me, making me shiver.

Supposing she did love me—what kind of love was it? I contemplated all the different shapes I could possibly imagine, but...eh, they all seemed pretty cool in their own unique ways. Really, they were all just variations of caring about someone and being kind to them, which was really admirable and stuff...

I just couldn't relate to it, that's all. I only knew how to be kind out of obligation.

"What am I gonna doooo...?" I sang as I went back inside my house. My flushed skin craved the caress of the electric fan.

After that, we talked on the phone all night long, and then I spent the entire next day thinking about the bath and the swimsuits and writhing in my room. Whenever I wore myself out, I'd sit and recharge for a while.

As I was watching TV and zoning out, a news program came on with a disturbing story about a student who snapped and killed someone after a heated argument. For a moment, I reflected on the fragility of human lives. Under a little pressure, just about anyone could commit murder. Not that *I* was planning to do anything like that, of course. But perhaps I was capable of more than I gave myself credit for. If I used that power to be a force for good, I could probably accomplish some pretty amazing things...

This filled me with a strange sense of courage, and I grabbed my phone. *It's basically nighttime now, right?* My gaze flickered up at the clock on the wall.

Truth be told, I wanted to talk for longer. I never wanted us to be apart. But social norms like "time" and "family" and "common sense" pulled her away from me, and my insecurities made me scared.

I still didn't know the truth about that other girl, and I still wanted answers. But I didn't want to keep obsessing over that mystery, nor did I want to exhaust all my energy on other people. Yes, I was afraid of Shimamura making other friends, and yes, I was afraid she liked them more than me. But those fears were an obstacle between me and her, and I wanted to come to terms with it. That way I could overcome it.

As I waited for her to answer my call, I amended my statement a tiny bit:

I want to spend so much time with her that the little changes don't even register on my radar.

Adachi was calling again. But we had already talked for hours last night—what more could she possibly have to say? Nevertheless, I picked up the phone.

"Th-there's something I forgot to say last night," she blurted out. No perfunctory greeting, just cutting to the chase at the speed of light and stumbling over herself the whole way there. This was the Adachi I knew.

"Go for it," I replied, prompting her to continue. *She's not going to profess her love for me like she did in the bathtub, is she? Probably not, right?* And yet I still braced myself just in case. I could hear her gripping the phone tightly on her end and pictured her leaning forward.

"Would you wanna...hang out...at the festival this weekend?"

"Oh, is *that* what this is about?" *Well, that was anticlimactic.*

"Wha? Huh?" she spluttered. "Wh-what else would there be?"

"Don't worry about it. Just talking to myself." *More like talking* about *myself,* I thought with a grin. "Anyway, sure, I don't mind."

"...You don't?" she asked timidly, like a scolded child.

"Well, I don't have plans with anyone else this time around." Thus, I had no reason to decline.

"What a relief...!"

She let out a heavy sigh that expressed precisely how worried she had been. Was it really that stressful of a question? From her perspective, probably. I didn't know for sure, but if I had to guess, she was most likely still hung up on the Tarumi incident. When I thought back to that super-emotional phone call, near the start when Adachi was still coherent, she was asking an awful lot about Tarumi.

Should I just explain it to her and get it over with? But how? Tell her Tarumi's an old friend with whom I recently... er...reconciled? Is that even the right word? It was all so complicated. This was probably why I kept putting it off in the first place.

"I was gonna ask you in person when I was at your house yesterday, but I kinda forgot..."

"Oh, right. Because you passed out."

At this, she faltered. If we were in the water, this little crab would probably be blowing bubbles all over again.

"You know, Adachi—" I began without thinking, then hastily stopped myself and averted my eyes. "On second thought, never mind."

"What is it?"

"Nothing." For once, *I* was struggling to continue the conversation.

"But I wanna know..."

"I'll tell you later, I promise. Now then, where should we meet up on the night of the festival?"

At the very least, I was more adept than Adachi at changing the subject. Not that it was anything to be proud of—I had spent more time dealing with people, so I had mastered all the most efficient techniques. But "efficient" was not the same as "good."

After we settled on a meetup spot and time, she hastily ended the call. Maybe she felt like she needed to start getting ready, even though the festival was still days away... *Nah, that can't be it,* I laughed to myself. But of course, when it came to Adachi, the possibility of her overthinking things was a permanent fixture.

So why on earth did I nearly ask her to describe the way in which she loved me?

I could already envision the sheer panic that would erupt in response to that kind of question. In fact, part of me wanted to see it unfold in person, which is why I decided not to ask over the phone... Did that make me an evil person?

There was just something *exhilarating* about the way she fought through her fears to take action. Watching her was like watching fireworks—she exploded in ways I'd otherwise never have the chance to see.

And when it came to Adachi Sakura, those sparks were always cherry-blossom pink.

I called Shimamura and told her I wanted to see her.

Adachi called and told me she wanted to see me, so I left the house.

I hunched my shoulders and tried to hold back my feelings as I yearned for Shimamura with all my heart.

Adachi...

Shimamura...

Even as the clock was running out on our summer vacation, the heat showed no signs of receding. This was something I found frustrating. If I was already miserable just sitting around my house, how was I supposed to find the motivation to go outside? Most days, I ended up twiddling my thumbs in my room. This was to be expected, however. People who tried to fill their vacation days with activities were completely missing the point. Vacations were supposed to be a *break*. Praise be to the blank calendar.

Unlike me, my little sister was downstairs in our room, calmly working on her homework. Hard to say if she actually felt as calm as she looked—it probably depended on the amount she had left to finish. But since she liked to play the part of a goody-goody honor student at school, she probably didn't have much more to do.

"Ah, I have discovered Shimamura-san!"

Then Yashiro walked in. When she spotted me, she beamed and toddled right over. This time, oddly enough, she was carrying her astronaut helmet under her arm. Only then did I remember that this kid was pretending to be an alien.

"I was hoping to enrich my friendship with Little, but she told me she is too busy with her homework."

"So she kicked you out, huh? Join the club."

Likewise, I had come up to the second-floor study room to let her work in peace. But I didn't have anything to do, and the air circulation was terrible up here, so my only oasis from the suffocating heat was an ancient electric fan. Its generated breeze wasn't even cold, but at least it kept the air from stagnating.

Yashiro set her helmet in the corner of the room, then came and sat between my legs. I was sitting right up against the table, but nevertheless, she wedged herself in. Her hair fluttered in the fan's breeze, tickling my face... For some reason, filling my vision with her cool color palette never failed to make me feel a bit chilly. Evidently, she was the perfect summer accessory.

"You said you don't have any homework, right? Because you don't go to school?"

"That is correct," she declared, thrusting out her chest.

I couldn't help but wonder about the circumstances behind it. Most kids her age were required by law to attend school, so it was a huge mystery. But even if I rattled her head around, I knew I'd never get an answer out of her. Maybe she really was an alien. Not like it would change anything.

"Do *you* have any of this 'homework,' Shimamura-san?"

"Of course I do." Believe me, I had plenty of it. And I was gonna get around to it...later. Probably.

Then I wondered how Adachi was doing with *her* homework. When we first met, she was a delinquent, so maybe she hadn't touched it...or maybe she'd already dutifully finished it. *It's not like she thought I was serious when I said we didn't have any, right?* Given her personality, I figured she had it all scheduled out. At her core, she was a very responsible girl. *It's just that she kinda loses her composure whenever I'm involved.*

Looking back, it was all so obvious. She often became flustered in social situations due to her critical lack of experience, but fundamentally, she wanted to improve herself and she wanted to be seen in a positive light. That was just how much she loved me... The thought made me blush.

My first instinct was to question whether maybe her love for me was all some misunderstanding on my part, but...most likely, it wasn't. That being said, I didn't actually know for sure what kind of love she felt for me, but being in love with someone generally meant you wanted to spend all your time with that person, and Adachi fit the bill. Her eyes, her attitude, her *entire vibe* begged to be with me. Whenever she panicked, she'd always get this complicated look on her face—it was practically her signature look at this point.

To be clear, I didn't mind spending time with her, but what was supposed to happen from there? Adachi seemed convinced that something else would come of it, or else she wouldn't angle for it constantly. What did she want from me? I could envision her asking me to *hold hands with her forever* and *stay with her forever* and *only ever think about her* and *never look at a single other person ever again*. Frankly, it all seemed so *exhausting*. I could handle living my life without other people, but the prospect of being stuck with only Adachi, forever and ever, was...not pleasant.

Besides, if I followed those instructions to the letter, then I wouldn't be myself anymore. At that point, would she still love me? What did she even love about me to begin with? If I asked her flat out, she might run for the hills. Alternatively, on the off chance that she *did* give me an answer, I could easily picture her saying, "Everything!" or something else equally as vague and unhelpful.

"Is something on your mind?" Yashiro asked suddenly, bringing me back to reality. I looked down to find two untainted blue globes looking back at me.

"Huh? You can tell?" *That's weird. I thought I was pretty zoned out.*

"Keh heh heh! I have X-ray vision!"

She opened her eyes as wide as they could go...but to me, her eyes just looked like regular old eyes, so I wasn't buying it. In fact, they were so pretty, I couldn't really take her seriously.

"You can talk to me about it if you'd like," she continued, fixing me with those big eyes. Given how wide she was stretching them, you'd think they'd be bloodshot, but nope. The whites of her eyes were as clear as a still lake, with her round sapphire irises seemingly floating on top. She was so flawless, I couldn't help but marvel at the fact that she was somehow a living, breathing person rather than a doll.

That being said, the thought of asking *Yashiro* for advice made me laugh out loud. Maybe if my problems involved doughnuts or something.

"Hey! I care about more than just doughnuts!" she protested, balling her soft little hands into fists and swinging them around with a smile.

I stared at her in shock. How could she have possibly known what I was thinking?

"I love all carbs equally!"

"...Yes, of course, sweetie."

I stroked her hair, and little blue light particles gently floated out from between my fingers. I could already tell this was going to go poorly, but I decided to ask her regardless.

"Why do you choose to be kind to people?"

A kid like her wouldn't have ulterior motives. Surely there was something else to it.

"Because I like you earthlings very much," she replied offhandedly, without missing a beat.

"Hmm." Once again, like with Iwaya-san, I had asked the wrong person.

"In particular, I especially like you and Little. I feel we share the same wavelength."

"I see."

Well, that was direct. I averted my eyes. I wasn't sure I understood what she meant by *wavelength*, but her unfiltered honesty made me squirm. That being said...the old me would have said this stuff too. Strange to think that growing up had somehow made me *less* capable than I was before.

"Do you like me, Shimamura-san?"

"Huh? Well, let's see... Eh, you're okay for a little kid." I'd probably say the same to my sister too, if she ever asked.

"Then that makes us friends!" Yashiro declared, beaming up at me as she rested against my chest. And when I looked back at her, I could feel my shoulders relaxing as a smile crept up on my face.

Her innocence was contagious and unlike anyone I'd ever known...which is to say that normally most people grew out of it. That was why my personality and priorities had changed, and when I saw Yashiro rejecting that transition, it made me...worried? Jealous? Nostalgic for the old days? All of the above, perhaps. Her purity slashed at my heart like a cat's claws. But she didn't realize this, of course.

"Mmmhh!"

When I stretched her cheeks, they *really* stretched. *Man, I could get addicted to this.* Then, as I was entertaining myself, my sister came upstairs to tell us she had finished her allotted quota of homework for the day.

"Hello there, Little."

"Did you finish your homework, kiddo?"

"Hmmm..." She frowned at each of us in turn. "I'll go with Yachi."

"Okay...?" For some reason, she chose Yashiro but not me.

Time passed, and I found myself wondering what they were up to. "Enriching their friendship" with snacks, if I had to guess. They were really getting along these days, as evidenced by the audacity with which Yashiro mooched from our family. Lately, she showed up for nearly every meal.

"Feels like she's gonna move in at this rate..."

And for some reason, no one in the family would take issue with it. Had she put us all under hypnosis or something? *Eh, whatever.* I didn't really have a problem with her. After all, blue was my favorite color.

Seeing as my sister had finished her homework, there

was no longer any need for me to camp out up here...but right as I was about to get up, my phone started ringing.

"Yes, yes, I hear you," I muttered as it blared. I figured it was Adachi again, but it was actually Tarumi. *That's unusual... Wait, no, it isn't.* Now that I thought about it, she called me quite a lot. As I stooped down in front of the noisy electric fan, I picked up.

"Hello? Taru-chan?"

"Sup, girl?"

"Not much..."

While my voice was lethargic in the heat, hers was chipper and lively. You'd think all delinquents were sullen and bratty, but not this one, apparently.

"Just thought I'd call since we haven't been able to talk in a while."

"We haven't?"

"I mean, like, I haven't been able to call you."

"Really? How come?"

"Well...whenever I try, usually the line's busy."

Her tone was passive-aggressive. For a moment I was confused, but then it sank in.

"I mean, not that I've been calling you *every day* or anything!" she continued hastily. "I must just have really bad timing or something."

"Something like that, I guess!" I nodded.

But in reality, it was probably because I spent so many hours on the phone with Adachi. I hadn't internalized it until now, so it was actually kind of a shock. I thought I had my friendships all figured out, so I never realized just how unbalanced things had gotten. But when I thought about it, yeah... These days, my attention was leaning pretty heavily in Adachi's favor.

"Wow..."

There was something almost remarkable about it—a sudden sense of freedom, like if a bad head cold had vanished in an instant. Or like I'd found a secret room behind a false wall in my house. It was exciting in a good way.

"What's up?" she asked.

"Umm..." How could I explain it? My gut was telling me not to go into detail, lest things get complicated.

Why, oh, why must it be so hard to manage my friendships?

If you played with one particular toy too much, your greasy little hands would make it all grimy—but if you didn't play with it *enough*, it would get dusty, and you might forget it was even there. *Moderation is key,* as the saying went, but when it came to finding that perfect middle ground, I struggled. If such a skill existed, then it wasn't in my wheelhouse. Frankly, I was just too lazy to care.

"Well, anyway...that's not what I wanted to talk about," she continued.

"Oh, yeah?"

"See, there's a festival this weekend... Actually, you probably already know about it, right? The festival this weekend?"

"Yeah...?"

"And I haven't seen you lately...or at least, not since you got back from your trip...so I was thinking it might be a good...opportunity..."

So that's *what this is about—an invitation to the festival.* But this time, Adachi had asked first, and I'd already agreed to go with her.

That being said, Tarumi wasn't like Adachi; if I invited her along as a third wheel, she'd probably be fine with it. In that case, we could enjoy the festival as a trio...right? *I don't know about that,* said a niggling little voice in the back of my head. *Adachi won't like it. What if it makes her cry?*

When I thought about it that way...

"I'm sorry." Mentally, I pressed a finger to the wet earth and drew a line in the sand. "But I already agreed to go with someone else."

On the other side of the gulf between us, I could hear a hint of panic in her breath. Her voice felt so far away.

"Oh, I...I see..."

"Yeah..."

I switched off the fan. I was worried maybe I jumped the gun in turning her down since I didn't let her finish talking, but it turned out I was right.

"Is it, like...your sister or something?"

"No, uh, a classmate from school."

It was the blandest word I could have possibly chosen to describe my relationship with Adachi. Surely I could have picked *anything* else—*friend, class-ditching buddy, fellow oddball.* This *classmate* and I had spent the past year building something special together and making it shine. She gave me so much, and somehow I never got tired of it...

"Oh, c-coo—cool, cool." Meanwhile, Tarumi cooed like a pigeon. But I could tell there was more she wanted to say.

"So, yeah...I can't."

I could have softened it and told her I wished I could go with her, but instead, I chose not to. I didn't fully grasp what this meant, nor did I see where it would lead. Regardless, I committed myself to widening the gulf.

"No can do, huh?"

No can do. The tension hung heavy in the air, but I felt no regret.

Thankfully, the call ended shortly after that. I sighed heavily, and my shoulders drooped. The weight of all these interpersonal relationships made my bones creak. Still, after I let out all my breath and stared at the floor for a while, I could feel a burden lifting. On second thought, perhaps we humans crammed a few too many things into our lives. Maybe it was that invisible weight that caused us to develop the terminal illness known as laziness.

I set my phone down and went downstairs. Then I heard noises coming from the kitchen, so I peeked inside. Sure enough, I found my mother dicing up an onion.

"Hey, Mom, would you lend me one of your yukatas later?"

"I beg your pardon?"

"I wanna wear one to the festival this weekend," I explained casually...and yet I could feel an ache in my chest. It was hard for me to outright ask for the things I wanted; it made me feel painfully vulnerable. This was a feeling I only started to experience after I hit double digits, and I hadn't struggled with it this hard in quite some time.

"Sure, no problem. So what changed your mind? Last time you weren't interested."

"Mmm, I just feel like it?"

She looked at me skeptically as she chopped her onion. Why did she always have to point out all the things

I didn't want her to notice? Maybe that was just how parents operated. They spent a lot of time with us, so they could easily detect every tiny change.

"Plus, last time I went, literally *everybody* was in a yukata except me."

"Ha ha ha! I tried to warn you, but you never listen!" she scoffed, as if she always knew everything. But of course, my dear mother never let a little thing like *compassion* slow her down. "So now you're going to *another* festival?"

"I got invited, so, yeah."

"You did, hmm?"

For some reason—maybe because I shot Tarumi down?—I felt strangely guilty.

"Anyway, thanks in advance," I blurted as I rushed out of the kitchen. I hadn't done anything wrong, nor had my mother, and yet once I was out of her line of sight, my pace quickened. My legs were restless, as if something was goading me on.

I hadn't lied to her. Everything I said back there was true. But there *was* one more reason, if you could call it that. More of an offhand whim, really.

I just thought it would make Adachi happy.

interlude **Hino Returns**

"Waaaah! Hinoooo!"

"I know, I know. You love me soooo much. There, there. Now let go of me."

Never in my wildest dreams did I imagine she'd be waiting in my room to ambush me the literal second I got home. *Seriously, don't cling to me while I'm in the middle of changing! I'm trying to take my clothes off, and no, I don't need your help, thanks!*

"It is I, Nagafuji, your faithful canine companion."

"Hey, *canine*, don't pinch my butt!"

"When I asked the maid, she let me right in! Weird how people always seem to remember me!" she exclaimed as she nuzzled her cheek against my butt. *Cut it out, you little twerp!*

"No, *you're* weird for forgetting people all the time!"

"Waaaah!"

"Oh, be quiet, you baby! Now let me get dressed!"

I kicked her off and sent her rolling to the floor. Surprisingly, she went without a fight; she must have gotten tired of clinging to me. But for some reason, her rolls were lopsided...almost like some part of her wasn't as flat as the rest... *On second thought, let's not go there. Good grief... And here I was planning to go to* your *place...*

"Did you have fun in Hawaii?"

"Eh, it was pretty average."

Except for that time one of the locals caught a shark with their bare hands and started screaming, "Dinnertime, woohoo!" But other than that, it was pretty uneventful—no walking around, except to go from the hotel to the private beach or the pool and back. Just another summer trip abroad, really.

Out in the hall, I could hear flustered footsteps racing this way and that, and every now and then, I caught a glimpse of one of my brothers in silhouette through the paper doors. Our family was so huge, it made coordinated travel a total nightmare—not just for the departure, but the return too. And since my brothers had brought their entire families, there were children screeching everywhere. This was precisely why I wanted to escape to

Nagafuji's house. But of course, this chick never took *my* feelings into consideration.

"You missed me that much, huh?"

"Of course I did!"

"Hmmm." I kept forgetting that kind of joke didn't work on her. Instead, it would only backfire, and my resulting embarrassment made it look like I wasn't joking at all.

As I pulled on my shirt, I could hear the cry of the cicadas on the other side of the paper door. Hawaii didn't have cicadas, so it was this sound that reminded me I was truly home again. Simultaneously, I felt a little thrill at the thought that I had left the confines of my country. Yes, bizarre though it was, I didn't get excited about traveling until after the trip was already over. But now that I was back home, the memories were vivid and bright. Maybe I just needed a little perspective to truly appreciate everything.

And so I finally finished changing, no thanks to Nagafuji, but then she had the nerve to complain: "That's not a kimono!"

"I'm not gonna wear all those stupid layers in the middle of summer!" Maybe once the weather cooled down. Not like Nagafuji was going anywhere anyway.

"Oh, that reminds me!" Just then, she started waving her hand in the air.

"What is it?"

"I wanna get a job at your house!"

"...*What*?" Usually I could understand the gist of what she meant whenever she spoke, but this time she left me utterly confused. A job? At my house? "What's that supposed to mean?"

"Well, I want to work at your house."

That's the part I don't get, genius. Our family business didn't hire outsiders, and even if we did, personality-wise, she wasn't cut out for that line of work. So what other "job" could she get at our house...? Marrying Goushirou?

No, no, no. Not happening. Absolutely not. For some reason, this pissed me off. *Explain yourself, damn it!* Fortunately, she sensed me glaring at her and started talking.

"I could be one of your family's helpers! Then we could see each other every day!"

"Oh, *that*... Noooo, no, no. Forget about it." I waved a dismissive hand.

"Whyzat?"

"Because you're useless!"

My family was only nice to her because she was a guest; they wouldn't tolerate her behavior if she was an employee. And besides, I did *not* want my stupid brothers or whoever else barking orders at her. The thought pissed me off even more. The Nagafuji I knew was a free spirit, and I wanted her to stay that way.

"No, I'm not. Everybody needs a Nagafuji!" she declared with a little dance, making her chest jiggle. I was not amused.

"Listen here, you..."

"Think about it, Hino! Every minute I spend without you is boring, and lonely, and a big fat waste of time!" She counted on one hand as she spoke. Although she only had three main points, she extended all five fingers and held them up like that was some kind of proof. "See? Nothing but downsides!"

Light shone through the paper doors onto her fingers, creating a shadow on the tatami floor like the hands of a clock. But those hands were stuck in place, immobile, like the endless summer season.

In Hawaii, time moved slowly. With every cool breeze, I could feel myself inching forward with the rest of the world. Japan's summers, however, felt stagnant, like an isolated dimension where the only thing that existed was *heat*. But sometimes, when I needed a moment to be lazy, that stillness was a comfort to me.

"So that's why—*waaaah*! Hinoooo!"

She seemed to remember something partway through, because she suddenly latched onto me. And the way she nuzzled her chin against my scalp, she really *was* acting like my pet dog.

She's so...

There in her arms, the thoughtless words wouldn't leave my lips.

"You feel kinda warm. Did you bring the Hawaii sunshine back home with you?"

"Something like that," I shrugged, playing it off.

Her pale wrists gleamed as she cradled my head. This was the one thing Hawaii didn't have. *But sure...let's go with what you said.*

"We have food stand at next festival. You help, okay?"

"I'm sorry, but I have plans that day," I replied, rejecting my manager's request. "Really important plans," I added. I was *not* going to let her talk me into this. Worst-case scenario, I was ready to quit if I had to.

"Hrrmmmm…"

She pretended to look worried, but then the other girl walked out wearing her *cheongsam*. Of course! Come to think of it, we had a new girl working here now!

"I'll let *you* handle this," I told her, bowing deeply.

Thus, I succeeded in dumping my shift on someone else instead. I refused to make this same mistake a second time. Now all possible obstacles between myself and my life's ambition had been eliminated.

Excellent.

5. Liftoff

EVERYTHING I'D WRITTEN DOWN was about Shimamura, so I called them my Shimamura Notes—short and to the point. Now I was preparing to add a new entry, and as my brain churned at the speed of light, I could feel the birth of a new sun taking place behind my eyes.

What did people do at summer festivals? I had very limited experience as an attendee. Frankly, I had "very limited experience" in most things; this was something I had become painfully aware of ever since I met Shimamura. And although I was trying to learn the ropes, I never managed to catch up in time. Instead, I fumbled my way through every crisis like the idiot I was.

Back on topic: festivals. What was the best way to get maximum enjoyment from one? Buy food from a food stand and watch fireworks? Hold hands and talk? What else? I couldn't think of anything.

But after a few days of mulling it over during my free time, I realized I was getting my hopes up *way* too high. It was just a festival; all we'd do is walk through it together. Granted, it would still be a lot of fun, but I needed to make sure I wasn't setting myself up for major disappointment afterward. As long as we smiled and ate food and watched the pretty fireworks, that was enough.

With that conclusion reached, I closed the notebook. If I let myself overthink this, I was only gonna screw it up. Instead, it might be nice to play it by ear without worrying too much. My past failures rose up in my mind one after another...and as I clutched my head and writhed, I could feel the sleeves of my yukata brushing against my skin.

After many, many attempts to get my outfit to cooperate, I was now dressed and ready to go, but there was still plenty of time before we were scheduled to meet up.

Outside my window, I could see the sun slowly wilting like a flower, pulling the blue sky along with it, its last few rays shining into my room. Once upon a time, the end of each day felt like merciful relief to me, but that was in the past, before I met Shimamura. Now that I was a different person, the setting sun sent a shiver down my spine.

My gaze darted restlessly from the window to the clock and back. Before long, I decided to forego the torture of sitting around in my room and head out to the meetup spot instead. Story of my life.

Before I left, I stood in front of the mirror and examined myself one last time. I had to look up instruction videos online to figure out how to tie my sash, so hopefully it looked okay. I turned from side to side, scrutinizing its position on my waist.

What about my hair? I wondered, grabbing a fistful. I hadn't styled it, and now that I was gearing up to leave, I was starting to second-guess myself. But every attempt at a different style looked like trash, so I kept putting it back, and I could already tell I was going to stand here forever if I didn't stop myself. *Better to play it safe,* I figured.

But as I stepped out into the hall, I could see a shadow... and it wasn't my own.

"Oh, my."

I had inadvertently crossed paths with my mother, who had finally come home from God knows where. She seemed surprised to see me in a yukata. We both tensed up, our movements stiff and reactive, like we were bound by invisible string.

"Going out?"

I nodded at the floor, my head bobbing lifelessly. "Yeah."

My stomach churned. I wanted nothing more than to flee. *Please hurry up and go away now.* None of these were things I was meant to feel toward my family... Sometimes I had to wonder why she gave birth to me at all. With my face downturned, I moved to walk past her.

"You'll look tacky with your hair down. Want me to braid it?"

At first, I thought I must have misheard. It was just so far-fetched. Meanwhile, she looked back at me, every bit as uncomfortable as I was. Then, finally, her suggestion sank in, and I remembered that this woman was technically my mother. My fingers curled into a tiny, tight fist.

"Okay."

She started walking, and I followed after her, both of us silent. I was intensely nervous, but not the same way I was around Shimamura. There was no electrical current running through my body—just constricting tension.

As I sat down in front of the mirror, I felt a weight press down on my shoulders. Likewise, my mother squinted timidly as she ran a comb through my hair. I nearly made eye contact with her reflection, but I hastily averted my gaze just in time. It was so unnerving, I could hardly breathe. Was this what "family" felt like for everyone? I hardly ever spoke to her, so I couldn't think of anything to say.

"Are you going with friends?" she asked suddenly as she picked up a hair tie.

"Ye..." I mumbled, barely audible. Then I cleared my throat and tried again, more firmly: "Yeah."

In the mirror, our eyes met for the first time in who knows how long.

"That's nice," she replied absently, averting her gaze, her body language matching mine. After that, she worked on my hair in silence until at last it was done. "There. Will that do?"

I touched my new side braid and nodded. "Yeah." Not like I could possibly tell her otherwise. I could still feel the tension in the air as I rose to my feet and headed to the door. Then I stepped into the *geta* sandals I'd bought specifically for this occasion and awkwardly grasped the door handle.

"Come home safe," her voice called after me, giving me a little push out the door. But when I looked over my shoulder, my mother had already disappeared into her bedroom.

I was so startled, I nearly tripped over my own two feet. As I straightened up, I could feel a response in the back of my throat...but instead, all I managed was a limp wave down the empty hallway.

I didn't expect this to be the start of anything new.

I knew it was too late for that. But maybe...just maybe...I was allowed to like it a tiny bit. Maybe now I could hold my head up high.

Out of habit, I grabbed my bike key before I left, but on second thought, I wouldn't be needing it tonight. At some point, I'd lost the charm that used to hang from my keychain, but I hadn't noticed until now—probably because I was always so focused on Shimamura. But even if my choices cost me something along the way, I would never regret choosing her. Right now, I firmly believed that I was making progress.

As I walked down the street, my gait grew lighter and lighter. So what if I was practically skipping? It was the night of the festival, and my spirits were high.

"Dooga shaka, dooga shaka! Vroom, vrooooom!"

Do you really have to make those noises while you do this?

Now that the sun was setting, the cicadas had fallen still. This was supposed to be the most peaceful time of day. And yet there we were in front of the vanity, my mother making weird sounds as she did my hair. *I regret ever agreeing to this.*

"Been a while since I last messed with your head, eh?"

"I think you mean 'with my hair,' Mom. Leave my head alone." *Unless you're gonna magically make me smarter. But knowing you, you'll probably tinker around in there like it's a Lego set.*

"Last time I did this for you, it was your junior high school graduation ceremony," she mused, pausing to place her hands on my head. "And now you're getting taller."

"Have I?"

"Oh, my baby's gotten so huge..."

Big, Mom. The word is "big." So much for our heartwarming family moment.

"All right, what if we swirl your hair in a spiral on top? Here's the windup—"

"Stop playing around!"

"Tsk... Fiiiine, I'll do something *normal*," she grumbled like a sulky child.

Next time I'm just gonna do my own hair...if there even is a next time.

The end result: a perfectly ordinary bun. I examined myself in the mirror and decided I was pretty satisfied. "Yeah, that's good enough."

"*Good enough*? Whatever. Gimme."

She held out her hand, palm up. I looked down at it in confusion.

"Thanks for coming to the Shimamura Salon. That'll be 3,000 yen."

"Ha ha ha ha!"

"Ha ha ha ha ha!"

"Hah hah hah!"

"Gah ha ha ha!"

But she refused to retract her hand. I shook my head in disbelief. And in the end, I caved. "Just, uh, put it on my tab."

"You got it."

And then she literally wrote it down. *Wow, you're really committed to this gag, huh? ...It is just a gag, right, Mom?* I decided to pretend I didn't notice.

Next, I wanted to double-check my yukata. It wasn't one that Yashiro or my sister had borrowed—it was white with a sunflower pattern and a blood-orange sash.

"You sure have a lot of these, huh?"

"Got 'em from Mom. Speaking of which, is it true you two are pen pals now?" she asked as she cleaned the stray hairs out of the comb.

"Oh, yeah. She sends me pics and videos of Gon," I replied, playing with my bangs.

"Ah, the dog. Right," she murmured absently. Then her tone shifted abruptly. "If his health starts failing, you should go out there and look after him."

I turned and looked over my shoulder at her.

"I'm happy to drive you," she continued casually, comb in hand.

"......"

"Hey! I can *see* you thinking rude thoughts about me! Look, I promise not to get mad, so just tell it to me straight."

"...I was surprised to hear you sounding like an actual mother for a change."

"Keeyoooo!" She started making weird noises again, but at the very least, she didn't seem angry. *Good grief, what a weirdo.*

I checked my hair one last time, then left the room, where I promptly encountered my little sister speed-walking down the hall.

"Ooh, you're wearing a yukata!"

She rushed over to me. Quietly, I began to dread what was going to happen next. Not like I could avoid my own sister at my own house, but ideally I was hoping to slip out while she was distracted.

"Are you going to another festival?"

"A friend invited me, so, yeah."

"Hmmm..."

She did *not* look pleased about this. I half-expected her to start demanding I take her with me. But Adachi wasn't Tarumi; she simply wasn't capable of tolerating a third (or fourth) wheel. Not that my sister seemed to like Adachi all that much anyway. *And festivals are for having fun, not fights.*

As I smiled stiffly, searching for a way out of this...

"All right then, how about you and I go together?" my mother offered to her, popping out of the bedroom like a life raft in the nick of time. Somewhere in that thoughtfulness, I caught a glimpse of Grandma.

"Really? You'll take me?"

"I'm acting like a real mom today!"

So you admit you're a bad mom the rest of the time?

Laughing, I rolled my eyes, but I wasn't annoyed at all. Likewise, my sister grinned up at her, delighted by the rare treat. It was actually a really nice moment, and while I don't think I could explain it eloquently, part of me wished it would last forever.

"How very exciting," said a head of blue hair that sprouted out from behind my sister. As usual, Yashiro was an utter enigma.

A pale pink flower-patterned yukata with a pale purple sash. Compared to everyone else who passed me on the street, I felt like I still looked tacky...or was I just paranoid? I had rushed out to buy this yukata immediately following the phone call with Shimamura, and I hadn't paid much attention to the pattern at the time, but now I was having doubts.

Maybe I should have asked her if she had any requests. Wait, but wouldn't that make me her dress-up doll?

I pictured Shimamura undressing me. Spreading me open like a fish. *Wait, what?*

"God, I'm so stupid...!" I buried my face in my hands in shame. If I wasn't in public, I'd probably be writhing right about now.

Our meetup spot was located just outside the hotel on the way to the fireworks venue. Apparently, the place was booked full of tourists, because groups of people in yukatas kept trickling out of the building and heading out to the river. The whole riverbank was now covered in visitors awaiting the fireworks...or at least, that was what people were saying online when I checked. But I didn't care about the fireworks. The prettiest thing I'd see tonight was going to be right beside me.

Is she here yet? Is she here yet? I glanced back down the street the way I'd come, scanning for any sign of her.

As the sunset faded, the town descended into the dark of night. The road was now a river of shadow, the pedestrians floating along like Bon Festival lanterns. But no matter how crowded the sidewalks grew, I was confident I would be able to spot Shimamura a mile away.

This festival wasn't as large as the one where I helped run the food stand, but nonetheless, I could feel excitement in the air. The people of this town took these events very seriously—possibly because there simply wasn't much else going on. Were they eager to see the fireworks? Or were they more interested in their companions? In my case, it probably went without saying.

Then, as I was shooing away the mosquitoes, my hand fell still.

"Oh...!"

Not even a supermodel could have looked better than she did. In an instant, she captivated me, and all else faded into the background. Never in my wildest dreams had I expected Shimamura to wear a yukata, and the impact made fireworks pop in my skull.

She waved at me; I waved back, then dashed over to her. I could feel my cheeks burning as I ran, but thankfully, it was so dark outside that she wouldn't be able to see me blushing. Hopefully.

When I came to a stop in front of her, she greeted me with a grin. She was wearing her hair in a bun, and her yukata had a flower pattern like mine, except with

a different type of flower. She looked so completely different, and yet it was unmistakably her... My brain was racing a hundred miles a minute, and I felt my whole face light up.

"You...you look so pretty!" I blurted out, no perfunctory greeting, before she had the chance to say a single word.

"Really?"

I nodded eagerly. "Really pretty!" Why did I keep repeating myself? Why was I so happy? It was a mystery.

"Well, that's flattering," she murmured, smiling, her gaze flitting to and fro. Then she looked up and clapped her hands together like she'd remembered something. "You look pretty too!" she continued belatedly, her smile deepening.

The instant I heard it, I could practically feel my ears melt. Sure, there was a noticeable pause, but what came next set off even *more* fireworks in my head. At this rate, I wouldn't even need the real deal.

Then Shimamura reached out to me, and my heart skipped a beat. As I watched, her fingers arrived at my braid. She pinched the end between her thumb and forefinger and lifted it up, wiggling the end like a little broom. "Cute braid. Did you do it yourself?"

Apparently, my new hairstyle really stood out since I

usually never did anything with it. "My...my mom did," I answered stiffly.

Naturally, Shimamura's eyes widened. "Whoaaa."

"Yeah."

"Wow..." Now she was acting a little *too* surprised. As far as I knew, she hadn't even *met* my mother.

"What about you?" I asked, gesturing to her bun. It made her look very...mature? Elegant? But at the same time, it was still cute.

"Oh, this? Yeah, my mom did mine for me too." She looked into my eyes, and we both smiled bashfully. "So, shall we get going?"

"Sure."

At her suggestion, the two of us started walking side by side, forming yet another swaying lantern in the river of people.

I snuck a peek at her calm, composed face in profile and felt my fingers spread on reflex. *Don't snatch, don't squeeze. Just be gentle.* I focused hard as I reached out—so hard, in fact, my hand started to tremble. As a result, I misjudged the amount of force I needed and inadvertently squeezed her hand too tight.

Ugh, not again! The feeling of failure made my vision go dim. But beyond a wry smile, Shimamura didn't seem all that bothered. "You're not very good at that, are you?"

"I'm sorry." But though I apologized, I wasn't about to let go. *Wait, what the?* I could feel a faint warmth on her palms that wasn't usually there. "Shimamura, were you holding hands with someone else just now?"

She looked at me sharply. "You can *tell*? That's actually pretty impressive. I take back what I said," she murmured in sincere amazement.

"Uh...well..." I backpedaled desperately. Was it creepy of me to notice?

"I was walking with my little sister until just now."

"Oh, I see..."

I was relieved to hear it wasn't some girl our age. Evidently, her little sister was somewhere around here too... Could I safely interpret her absence as a sign that Shimamura had chosen to prioritize me instead? I struggled to suppress my glee. If I'd won out over a family member, then...well...that was a big deal! I didn't have the words to describe it.

As I was floating along on cloud nine, Shimamura turned her whole body toward me and took my free hand in hers.

"Wh-what?"

"What about this one? Does it feel colder?"

"Yeah." The only warmth I felt was that of Shimamura herself.

"Whoa... Man, I really have to wonder if she's even human," she mused, tilting her head with a smile. Who was she talking about? "Anyway, I see you're early again, Ms. Punctual!"

Does it still count as punctual if I'm early, though?

"But this presents us with a problem," she continued.

"It does?"

She grinned. "Why, it would appear there's still time before the fireworks are scheduled to begin, my dear."

"Oh, *that*. That's no big deal." Because it meant I got to spend extra time with her.

In place of a proper response, I laced my fingers with hers, and a beat later, I felt her arm relax. Then we walked until we approached the bridge.

Here, food stands had sprouted up along the road, which was clogged with crowds. I really didn't realize just how packed these festivals were until I was on *this* side of the cash register. Like rouge upon a lady's cheek, the paper lanterns added a modest hint of color to the night.

"Is your Chinese restaurant running a stand tonight?"

"Yeah. Oh, but I don't have to work tonight, so don't worry," I explained, waving a dismissive hand.

"That's a relief," she nodded, chuckling for some reason.

Well, where to now?

As I contemplated our next destination, I heard a familiar voice in the distance cry out: "This watermelon tastes like *destiny*!" Why did I recognize that voice...? I looked around until I spotted little blue particles of light rising into the sky amid the crowd.

"Uh...l-let's go this way," I declared, pointing in the opposite direction.

"Sure," Shimamura nodded without argument. And so off we went.

Then, as we walked along the food stands, *another* familiar voice called out: "Hey there, come on down! How about some takoyaki? Hey, hey, hey!"

Inadvertently, this caught our attention. My jaw dropped—and for some reason, Shimamura's did too.

It was the fortune-teller from forever ago, beckoning to us from behind a food stand. Despite the faint light of the lanterns, I could see her bright red cheeks plain as day. But Shimamura seemed to recognize her too— how did they know each other? I couldn't really picture *Shimamura* of all people consulting a fortune-teller for advice. Oh, but then again, she said she watched that one horoscope show on TV, so maybe she was more interested in astrology stuff than I realized. Maybe that was something we had in common.

"Did your girlfriend get a new haircut?" the woman asked in a singsong voice, though her expression remained stoic.

Girlfriend? Girlfriend?! Likewise, Shimamura stared back wide-eyed.

"What, you kids don't listen to Kamon Tatsuo these days? *Hana kara Gyunyu*! Look it up!" She waved her hand as if to dismiss the topic entirely. "Anyway...hmm. I think I see what's going on here."

She looked from me to Shimamura and back, her eyes sparkling mischievously. *What do you mean, "What's going on here"?* For a split second, I was confused, but then it hit me: I had confided in this fortune-teller. She knew my secrets. I began to panic so hard, I actually let go of Shimamura's hand.

"Do you know her, Adachi?"

"Not really—anyway—what about you?" I asked, trying to play it cool, but belatedly realized I was talking *way* too fast. My neck felt like it was on fire.

"She hassled me the last time I was here."

"She hassled you?" I repeated, looking back at the fortune-teller. I was terrified that she was about to open her big fat mouth and blab to Shimamura.

The woman looked back at me and laughed loudly. "Relax, darling! I believe in client confidentiality!"

For a moment, I was relieved, but then I scowled. *If you really believed in it, you wouldn't have said that!*

Sure enough, Shimamura perked up. "Client confidentiality? About what?"

Argh! So much for "confidential"! "Uhhhh... Gosh, something sure smells good over here!" I said in a loud, forced voice, trying to change the subject while knowing full well it wouldn't sound natural. Stiffly, I walked right up to the fortune-teller's stand. *Why would a fortune-teller sell food anyway?*

Shimamura walked up beside me and peered at the woman's wares, looking perplexed. "The sign says *takoyaki*, but..."

Needless to say, the awkward hesitation there was entirely warranted, for the fortune-teller was apparently grilling fish-shaped *taiyaki* cakes instead. But while *taiyaki* cakes were usually plump, these were *unnaturally* bulky, like the filling was threatening to spill out at any moment.

"That sure doesn't look like *takoyaki*..."

"I assure you, they're filled with octopus this time."

"What?"

The woman picked up a fresh *taiyaki*, bit off its fish-shaped head, and showed us the filling. Sure enough, there was so much octopus meat inside, it was practically popping out. This explained why the outside looked so lumpy... The sight was enough to give me indigestion just thinking about it.

"After I skimped on the filling for the Fortune Takoyaki, I ended up with too much octopus left over," she shrugged.

Reflexively, Shimamura and I exchanged a glance.

"Feast your eyes on this creative innovation! Imagine all the disappointed children!" the fortune-teller continued, like it was a sales pitch. At this, Shimamura grabbed my hand without another word.

"Whoa!"

"From now on, try not to make eye contact with weirdos, okay?" she chided me as she dragged me away.

"Awww!" I could hear the woman lamenting behind us.

Shimamura started walking faster—but still not as fast as my heartbeat. Thanks to the fortune-teller, I was holding hands with Shimamura again... I mean, yeah, we were already holding hands earlier, but still! This time *she* initiated it, and that was important.

"Come to think of it, that lady told me she specializes in palmistry," Shimamura mused quietly to herself. "Did you have her read your palm or something?"

She shot me a sidelong glance. I didn't want to lie to her, so I conceded. "Yeah, one time, a long time ago. But just once," I pressed, holding up an index finger.

"Do you really need to emphasize that?" she asked, blinking. *Maybe not.* "So what was your horoscope? What'd she say?"

"Uhhh…" I thought back to the last time I saw that woman and all the screaming she made me do. "It wasn't about what *she* said, but what she made *me* say, I guess?"

"Huh?"

"What about some normal *takoyaki*?! Would you buy that?!"

"AAAGH!"

The fortune-teller had caught up to us, carrying a plastic to-go container and walking so fast, she was in danger of shooting straight past us. Why was she so persistent?!

"See, they're round this time! Normal, round *takoyaki*! So how about it?"

"Fine, fine! I'll buy it!" Shimamura sighed reluctantly, and I could hear the silent implication: *So you'd better leave us alone!*

"Thank you, come again!" the woman shouted automatically as she raced back to her food stand. But I could feel her watching me, and when I looked over, she thrust her fist into the air in a show of support.

Mind your own business! I thought as I waved at her dismissively. But at the same time, the thought that she could see right through me made a cold sweat trickle down my spine. Was it really that obvious? I looked down at our joined hands. *Yeah, I guess it is.*

"So anyway, what did she—"

"Oh, look over there! It's, uh...c-candy apples!"

Speaking of *obvious*, my subject changes weren't fooling anyone, but that didn't stop me. I forced my way to the candy apple stand. Truth be told, I'd never actually eaten one of these, though I'd heard of them. Then the guy asked me what flavor I wanted, but I didn't know they *had* flavors, so I just told him to give me whatever.

"Wow, it's as red as your face!" Shimamura commented next to me, and I could feel my cheeks proving her exactly right. Then she took the apple from my hands, and after a pause... "So what did your horoscope say?"

"Look! *Okonomiyaki* pancakes!"

You can probably guess what happened next. Then, right after I completed my purchase, Shimamura grinned. "Let's talk about astrology!"

"Uh...one water balloon, please!"

Boing, boing.

"C'mon, Adachi-chan, I wanna know about your horoscope!"

"Rrrgh!" I looked at her reproachfully. Even *I* was smart enough to put two and two together by this point. "Are you messing with me?"

"It's a lot of fun!" she replied, smiling brightly...and because she seemed so happy about it, I very nearly forgave her. Meanwhile, she tossed the water balloon in one hand. *Glad you like it, I guess.*

Unfortunately, we had now purchased far more food than we were capable of eating while walking.

"I wonder if there's any seating anywhere," she mused, craning her neck around as she held the container of *takoyaki*. At this point, we couldn't hold hands anymore, which meant I now had a vested interest in eating this food as quickly as possible.

"There's a park over that way," I suggested. Naturally, I had already scouted the place out in advance—which was my way of saying I'd gotten impatient and milled around here for a while yesterday.

"Lead the way!" she declared. So off we went.

It was so pathetically childish, even a *literal child* would laugh at me if I told them, but...I really liked it when Shimamura relied on me for this stuff. For a few precious seconds, it filled me with a sense of pride I otherwise never experienced. And so, with my head held a tiny bit higher than usual, I guided her to the park.

As we moved away from the bridge, the plants and trees grew in more thickly, blocking out the light from the lanterns. I thought maybe it would block out some of the heat and noise from the crowd, but no. A ton of people were at the park too.

Luckily for us, a straight couple had just vacated one of the benches; we walked past them on their way out, then sat down in their spot. Evidently, it was nearly time for the fireworks show, because people were starting to migrate to the edge of the park facing the river. I couldn't see much in the absence of the lantern lights, but I could vaguely make out a *lot* of silhouettes—maybe even more than the number of cicadas clinging to the trees.

Incidentally, there were plenty of other girls hanging out in pairs like us. For some reason, this came as a relief.

"What should we eat first?" Shimamura asked, eyeing the candy apple and *takoyaki* in turn.

"Okay, um...how about the *takoyaki*?" I suggested, opting for the one I'd eaten before. I took the container from her, then picked up one of the octopus dumplings by the toothpick.

It was too hot to eat whole, so I blew on it, then bit it in half. We didn't get to request any particular flavor, but from what I could tell, it tasted like soy sauce. As I chewed, however, I quickly sensed that something was wrong.

"What the?" I examined the half I hadn't eaten yet.

"What's wrong?"

"There's no octopus in this..."

I could see green onions, at least, but these "octopus dumplings" had approximately zero octopus inside.

"Are you kidding me? But she said she had extra!" Shimamura stared down at it, baffled. Then, after a moment, she laughed wryly. "Oh, *now* I get it."

"What?"

"She used all her 'extra' octopus in those stupid *taiyaki* cakes, so she probably didn't have any to put back in the *takoyaki*."

"Ha ha ha..." I laughed dryly. But if this was a joke, it wasn't funny.

I ate a few more dumplings; aside from the lack of octopus, they were bland, but otherwise edible. Once I'd eaten half the container, Shimamura traded me the candy apple, which she had already taken a few bites of. I could see that it was coated in some sort of bright red syrup—so bright, it was frankly overwhelming.

"Whoa. So candy apples really *are* apples," I mused quietly.

"Oh, my god, you didn't know?"

I scrutinized the spot where Shimamura had nibbled. Not that it really, you know, *mattered* by this point. We had shared plenty of drinks in the past. *Yeah, it's no big deal,* I told myself as I gingerly pressed my lips to the apple...engulfed in bittersweet agony all the while.

As for the *okonomiyaki*, we shared that too—though I ate a bit more of it than she did. By the time we were full, the crowd had swelled even larger, like a fruit on the cusp of ripening. Soon, the fireworks would begin.

"Are you having fun, Adachi?" Shimamura asked as she played with the water balloon. *What a silly question.* Whenever it was just the two of us, my spirits bounced higher than any old balloon.

"Yeah."

"Then that's all that matters."

She grinned from ear to ear, and her youthful innocence stirred something in my chest. "What about you, Shimamura?" I asked in return.

"Yep, I'm having fun," she replied promptly, as if she'd expected me to ask. "See?"

She bounced the water balloon higher and higher, and I started to wonder if all she cared about was her new toy. Part of me was relieved that she was enjoying herself, but the lingering anxiety was still there, barely suppressed beneath the surface. For a moment, I debated whether to ask her outright...but despite my fear, I just couldn't stop myself.

"More fun than...l-last time?" I asked, placing all my hopes on the water balloon as it bounced up and down. I wanted the time she spent with me to be better than any time she spent with other girls.

She smiled gently. "Maybe so." Then she ran a reassuring hand over my head. But it felt like she was just placating me, so this ultimately did nothing to quell my fears.

Still, I was done crying and throwing a fit about it. I needed time to cool my head, so I rose from the bench and walked away. "I'll go get rid of the trash."

"Aww, that's so thoughtful! Thank you."

Leaving Shimamura behind on the bench, I jogged over to the nearest trash can. Discarded trash littered the ground nearby, probably from lazy throws. At first, I figured I'd just ignore it, but it kept gnawing at me, so I caved and started picking it all up. Not that I believed in God or anything, but something told me my dreams wouldn't come true unless I earned them. I was no good Samaritan; I was just doing it for my own benefit.

By the time I finished my volunteer work, my steaming face had cooled off a bit, so I turned back toward our bench. In the distance, I could see Shimamura happily bouncing her water balloon. And as I admired her from a distance, I suddenly remembered: she didn't wear a yukata to the other festival.

Am I totally full of myself, or...is she wearing it just for me?

She spotted me and tilted her head. "Why are you just standing there?"

I felt my breath hitch in the back of my throat, then choked it back down. "I was just...noticing how pretty you look."

"Oh... Thanks."

Miraculously, I actually played it off pretty cool this time. *Go, me!* I could feel my veins pulsing in my neck.

Then she clapped her hands together and smiled, just like last time. "You look pretty too!"

"Th-thanks...!"

But we already had this conversation once before, so it wasn't as impactful this time around. Was it too entitled of me to hope for something new?

"Ooh, fireworks!"

She hopped to her feet and pointed out at the sky, where little red sparks scattered in all directions, carving a blossoming flower into the night. Before now, I had only ever heard them pop and crackle in the distance, so the heavy *BOOM* came as a real surprise, resonating deep in my chest.

"Wow...!" Shimamura murmured in awe.

A beat later, the crowd cheered, and more fireworks shot up.

"Cardinal red! Dark crimson! And finally, burnt sienna!" she exclaimed gleefully. I didn't really understand it, but apparently, she was enjoying all the different shades of red.

The crowd kept edging closer and closer to the river like they were drawn in by the fireworks. But I wasn't looking at the sky at all—I was more captivated by Shimamura. The multicolored glow afforded her a magical, ethereal beauty that penetrated my skin, my organs, my tear ducts, stirring me to life until all my purest emotions began to spill forth unhindered...and my only thought was that I wanted to tell her. Something inside me was crying out, begging to be heard.

Spurred on by the glittering lights, my shoulders swelled, and my feelings flared up with the fireworks.

"I LOVE YOU!"

It sounded like a romantic confession. Adachi's feelings blossomed with the fireworks, sending a shower of sparks raining down onto me.

I turned away from the sky and looked back at her. Beneath the rainbow of colored lights, I could see her frozen stock-still, mouth agape... Was she waiting for an answer?

Ugh, this is awkward. So, so awkward.

"Well...thank you very much!"

It was a pretty pathetic response, but I wasn't sure

what else I was supposed to say. Still, it seemed to resonate with her, because her expression shifted rapidly, like the fireworks above. Apparently, I'd snapped her back to her senses.

"Oh, man, you should see your face right now."

Where else would I have the chance to see Green Adachi or Orange Adachi? Amused, I stepped closer to get a better look...but she took a step backward. Then a second. Then a third. Her face sort of quimbled—you know, quivered plus trembled—and then she bolted.

"Hey, where are you—?!" *Going...*

It felt like this kept happening. First that one time at my house, and then a few other times since. I wanted to tell her it wasn't safe to run through a crowd, but she was now too far away to hear me.

She ran full-speed in the opposite direction of the festival, like she was trying to disappear into the dark night. *Stop! Stop!* But the flow of time didn't heed me, and neither did Adachi. All I could do was run after her myself. Meanwhile, the rumbling explosions faded into the distance.

Once we arrived back outside the hotel where we first met up, she finally slowed to a stop. Then she sank to the ground so hard, I almost thought she fell. By the time I caught up to her, my sandals had rubbed the skin between my toes completely raw, but I ignored it. Instead, I raced around in front of her, and she looked up at me with that candy-apple face of hers. This was the Red Adachi I was accustomed to.

"C'mon. Your yukata will get dirty," I told her as I offered her my hand.

Timidly, she reached out; I grabbed her and pulled her up. By the time she was back on her feet, however, she was well on her way to Blue Adachi. Her expression swayed like a ship on rough seas.

"Let's calm down, okay?"

I put a hand on her shoulder and moved her over to the corner of the building. No one else was around, since they were all busy watching fireworks. But fireworks were the least of my worries right now.

"Feeling better now?" I asked, though I knew it was probably too much to expect of her right now.

"Hhhh..."

Her jaw quavered. It wasn't much of an answer, but at least she was composed enough to respond to me at all. Her explosion had drowned out all the fireworks, and now she was threatening to detonate all over again.

First, I started with a warning: "It's really not safe to run off. There's too many people here...and there's cars and stuff, you know?"

The whole time I was chasing her, I was terrified that she might get hurt.

She shrank into herself as though I'd smacked her over the head. "I'm sorry," she apologized. Now I felt less like her sister and more like her mother.

"Good. Now, uh...it sounds like you...want to talk about something...right?" For some reason, I couldn't bring myself to be direct.

Her lips wobbled like she was holding in a sneeze. "I... I l..."

"Island?"

She shook her head aggressively. *Ugh, why did I think it was "island"? I'm so stupid.* I could feel my heart starting to race, but was I excited or scared? Either way, this was uncharted territory for me.

"I lo..."

She was trying to say something, but she kept stumbling. Tears sprang to her eyes—maybe she bit her tongue. But before I could ask if she was okay—

"I...I love you! *I love you!*" she shouted at me, and under the light of the fireworks, I could see the blood from her bitten tongue leaving her lips in a fine mist.

Never did I imagine I'd receive such a raw, coppery confession. It was a rather vivid experience, and not just visually. Add in the warm glow of the summer festival, and I was starting to feel dizzy. It was just so surreal.

"Right. Got it," I nodded.

Her face shifted to a silent, plaintive *That's it?* expression.

"Look, just give me a minute to think."

It was too sudden; my emotions had yet to catch up. I folded my arms in careful contemplation. But with Adachi visibly trembling right in front of me, I couldn't exactly focus. She was so tense, she was idling like a car... and yet for some reason, whenever she was in a heightened emotional state, it helped me keep my cool.

"Okay, so you love me. What is it you want me to do about it?"

At this, she flinched hard. Then she stared down at the ground and quietly voiced her demands. "Spend time with me?"

"I'm right here."

"Think about me?"

"I *do* think about you."

She whipped her head up to look at me, almost like she was shaking her bangs out of her eyes. Her damp eyes shimmered like the midday sun. "And only care about me."

"...Uhhhh..."

We were doing so well at the beginning too. But now she wanted me to care *only* about her? When I added it all together, what I got was...

"So...you want to be my girlfriend?"

Her shoulders shook, and I could see sweat beading on her scalp—but to her credit, things *were* getting pretty heated. Then she froze, unblinking, like she was struggling to parse it all. So I waited for her to make her decision, and at last, she nodded quietly.

Setting aside all the needless chasing and blood-speckled shouting, it was a short and simple request: *Please date me.* But what would it mean to form that kind of relationship with Adachi? We were both girls, and girls didn't normally date each other. So if a normal person saw us together, they'd think it was weird. Granted, Adachi wasn't the type to care about what other people thought... but what about me?

If everyone around us cast dirty looks at us, would I have the courage to keep holding her hand? If I truly loved her, I could endure it, right?

Romantic relationships were normally guy-girl pairs. But I wasn't trying to have babies at this age, so did my partner really *need* to be male? Surely there was more to love than that. Human connections were not simple checklists.

Looking back, I could finally admit it: I loved Gon. But I didn't decide to feel that way because I stood to profit from it—I just *loved* him. His fur, his personality, every little thing about him. Love was something that struck without warning, with no time for planning or bargaining in between. That was probably how it worked for Adachi too. And I wanted to respect that.

If I agreed to date her, we'd probably hold hands and go on dates... *Wait, but is that any different from what we already do?*

"...No..."

When I realized just how little would functionally change between us, it came as such a relief. It felt like I could really see the bigger picture.

"I guess it'd be pretty weird, huh?" Adachi murmured, trying to gauge my reaction. She looked up at me like a scolded puppy, her braid swaying. All in all, it was very cute.

"Yep."

"...So you're not comfortable with it, or...?"

I wasn't sure how to respond. What exactly was the "it" in this equation? Society's view of us, or...?

"Nah."

Her face fell so quickly, she seemed to almost shut down. After Orange Adachi came Blue Adachi. Very pretty, of course, but not how I wanted this to end.

"I'm saying I'll be *fine*," I clarified, realizing she had misinterpreted my response.

I was tired of overthinking this, so instead I touched her. Looked at her.

My heart went out to her. There was no part of her I couldn't find comfort in.

As her sorrow melted away, I looked up at the night sky. The darkness had permeated all the world's nooks and crannies, and no amount of fireworks would help us illuminate the other side. What awaited us there? Only time would tell. Tomorrow, I'd have to think about all sorts of mind-numbingly complicated things, but for tonight...

"Sure, why not?"

BOOM! A firework exploded over us, drowning out my answer.

And so I decided to try out a relationship with Adachi.

Afterword

I HAD A DREAM that every word I wrote had a typo in it. Alas, my brain doesn't have spell check.

Hello, Hitoma Iruma here. As I'm writing this, it's currently wintertime, and it's getting pretty cold. I don't know what season this book will be published in, but if it's not winter for you, then lucky you! I actually don't mind the cold that much, comparatively speaking, but it's hard to type when my fingers go numb. Nothing I can really do about it. Kinda feels like that White Album stand fight in *JoJo's Bizarre Adventure*.

Anyway! *Adachi and Shimamura* has now made it to six volumes! I haven't planned how much more I'll write, but rest assured that this isn't the final book. I hope you'll look forward to the next one.

Also, on an unrelated note: Will any of my readers recognize where I got Hino's and Nagafuji's first names from? I lifted a few other names from that game too. But of course, this story is nothing like that one...

I'd like to thank my former managing editor during *Adachi and Shimamura*'s publication in *Dengeki Bunko Magazine*—a truly genuine man with a longer intro section than any of the authors. I'd also like to thank my mother and father, the latter of whom has transformed into a very doting grandfather. Also, a big thank you to Non-san and my current editor... So, yeah, thanks, everybody.

—Hitoma Iruma